SUPERGRANNY

THE GHOST OF HEIDELBERG CASTLE

Look out, Europe!

Supergranny and gang are off to Germany and another roaring adventure. Supergranny scarcely lands her Gulfstream jet at Frankfurt International Airport before trouble breaks out at Heidelberg Castle.

Is the romantic old castle really haunted by the ghost of a beautiful princess?

Or have Supergranny, the Poindexter kids, Shackleford and that spoiled but lovable robot, Chesterton, flown smack into the scam of the century?

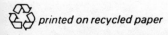

Supergranny Mysteries

Supergranny 1: The Mystery of the Shrunken Heads
ISBN 0-916761-16-9
Library Hardcover: ISBN 0-916761-17-7

Supergranny 2: The Case of The Riverboat Riverbelle
ISBN 0-916761-08-8
Library Hardcover: ISBN 0-916761-09-6

Supergranny 3: The Ghost of Heidelberg Castle
ISBN 0-916761-20-7
Library Hardcover: ISBN 0-916761-21-5

Supergranny 4: The Secret of Devil Mountain
ISBN 0-916761-04-5
Library Hardcover: ISBN 0-916761-05-3

Supergranny 5: The Character Who Came to Life
ISBN 0-916761-18-5
Library Hardcover: ISBN 0-916761-19-3

Supergranny 6: The Great College Caper
ISBN 0-916761-14-2
Library Hardcover: ISBN 0-916761-15-0

Buy Supergranny mysteries at your local bookstore, or ask the bookstore to order them. Or order them yourself with this coupon.

Holderby & Bierce, Publishing
P.O. Box 4296
Rock Island, IL 61201-4296

Please send the Supergranny mysteries checked above. Enclosed is my check or money order for $_____ ($3.25 for each paperback, $9.95 for each hardcover; plus $1.50 postage and handling per order.)

Name _____

Address _____

City _____ State _____ Zip _____

Allow 2 weeks for delivery.
Prices subject to change and offer to withdrawal without notice.

SUPERGRANNY

THE GHOST
OF HEIDELBERG CASTLE

Beverly Hennen Van Hook

Holderby & Bierce

Published by Holderby & Bierce, P.O. Box 4296,
Rock Island, IL 61201-4296

Andrea Nelken, editor

Paperback: ISBN 0-916761-20-7
Library Hardcover: ISBN 0-916761-21-5

SUMMARY: Has Elizabeth, the English princess who lived with her German prince
in Heidelberg Castle 350 years ago, returned to haunt the castle? Or is her ghost
a million-dollar scam created by slippery Count Otto von Bombast? Supergranny
and friends fly to Germany and investigate. Third in the series about the elderly
detective who drives a red Ferrari and fights crime.

Holderby & Bierce, October, 1987
2nd Printing, November, 1988
3rd Printing, March, 1993

Printed in the U.S.A.

To Don, Andi, Jamie and Ali and our good times together in Heidelberg . . . and to Wilhelmsfeld with love.

What about the *Real* Princess Elizabeth?

Everything in Angela's report about Princess Elizabeth — falling in love with Prince Frederick at sixteen; the humongous wedding in 1613 thrown by her father, King James I of England; her life at Heidelberg Castle; the Thirty Years War and even Jack the Monkey — is true, according to historical accounts of the times.

Drawing by Catherine Wayson after a portrait of Elizabeth.

It was 10 o'clock the morning after I'd walked across the Atlantic Ocean, and I was still pooped from the trip.

I hadn't actually walked across the water, you understand. I'd walked across the sky.

Forty thousand feet in the air, I had walked up and down the aisle of Supergranny's Gulfstream jet, stopping in the cockpit every ten minutes or so in hopes she would let me take another turn at the controls.

Supergranny and her cousin Carl, copilot on our flight to Germany, had let me take the controls for about two minutes right after we flew over Iceland, and it had revved me up too much to sleep.

My older sister, Angela, had studied her German phrase book for a while, then stretched out in a lounge chair to sleep. Meanwhile, my younger sister, Vannie, and our Old

English sheepdog, Shackleford, curled up in Supergranny's bedroom in the tail. Even Chesterton, Supergranny's hyper mini-robot, had finally unwound enough to crawl under a seat and shut off his lights and beeper.

Not me. I paced on, enjoying the thought of myself flying through the moonlit night to Europe. It paid off, because at dawn when I poked my head in the cockpit for the ninety-seventh time, Supergranny let me have another turn at the controls.

We arrived at Germany's Frankfurt Airport about 8 a.m., cleared customs and glided on the moving sidewalks to the main terminal. There we dropped our bags in a heap to say goodbye to Carl.

"See you here next week," he said, already dashing toward the door. *"Auf Wiedersehen . . . "*[1]

"Oh, brother," Supergranny whispered, shaking her head as he left. "I hope he's not disappointed. He's off to visit his old girlfriend Waltrop in Frankfurt, you know. Hasn't seen her since he was here in the Army thirty years ago." She shook her head again. "Sometimes these things don't go well."

"Don't worry, Supergranny," Vannie said, patting her hand. "Carl can take care of himself."

"He'll be all right," Angela added. "After all, he *is* 52 years old."

"I suppose you're right," Supergranny said. "At any rate, there's nothing we can do about it. Youngsters must lead their own lives."

I didn't consider Carl much of a youngster, but I man-

---

1. *Auf Wiedersehen*. Sounds like "Owf Veder sayin'." Means "Goodbye" (actually, "until we meet again").

aged not to say so. "Where's the surprise?" I said instead. Supergranny had promised us a surprise at Frankfurt Airport.

She laughed. "Follow me. Travel Formation 532X."

Travel Formation 532X means that Supergranny leads, carrying the large flight bag and pulling the two-suiter suitcase on wheels. Angela follows with the camera equipment, maps, hair dryers and Chesterton in her tote. Vannie follows with the snacks and Shackleford on a tight leash, and I bring up the rear with the other two suitcases. On top of all that, we all wear backpacks. We do *not* travel light, which is one reason we travel in formation.

"It will help cut down the confusion," Supergranny said. "I hope."

The black and white, gleaming and wonderful surprise was waiting outside at the curb.

"Whoa!" Angela exlaimed, dropping the hair dryers. "Whoa!"

"What *IS* it?" Vannie asked.

"A Porsche," I said calmly. "A Porsche," I repeated, less calmly. "A PORSCHE, A PORSCHE, A PORSCHE," I screamed, jumping up and down on the sidewalk.

Back in the States we always rode around in Supergranny's red Ferrari, but we had to leave it at home.

"I knew you were a little sad about leaving the Ferrari," Supergranny said, stowing our bags in the trunk. "And since I had to rent a car anyway, I figured I might as well rent something interesting. Do you think it will do for a week?"

"Oh, yes!" Angela said.

"You bet," Vannie said.

And what did I say?

3

"A PORSCHE, A PORSCHE, A PORSCHE," I screamed, still jumping up and down.

We drove south on the German autobahn, then followed a narrow, winding road up into the forested hills called "The Odenwald" to the village of Oberunterdorf.

And here we were at 10 a.m., surrounded by flower boxes and sunshine on the balcony of the Oberunterhof guest house.

The reason we were in Germany was wrapped in a light blanket on Supergranny's lap. It was laughing and gurgling at Supergranny, who was busy laughing and gurgling back at it and saying things like, "Yesss, her Auntie Sadie is here . . . yesss, her is so sweet . . . yessss, her is . . . tut, tut, tut."

Actually, I shouldn't call it "it." It was a her, a she, a girl. She was Supergranny's new great-niece, Sadie Geraldine Jr., named after the great Supergranny herself. (Supergranny's real name is Sadie Geraldine Oglepop.)

As soon as Supergranny had heard about the baby's birth, she had started coaxing our parents to let us fly to Germany to see her.

We live right next door to Supergranny, and our parents are good friends with her now, so she didn't really have to coax very hard.

And, of course, we'd done our part.

Angela had pointed out how educational the trip would be, I had cut the grass and carried out the trash without being asked and Vannie had handled the whining and wheedling.

We were staying at the Oberunterhof guest house, which was owned by Baby Sadie's parents and grandmother. Meg, Baby Sadie's mother, was Supergranny's American niece. She had met Rolf, her German husband, in college.

Right now, Meg and Rolf were busy setting up the guest house restaurant for lunch, but Oma, Rolf's mother, sat on the balcony with us.

Oma was a sturdy, red-cheeked, laughing woman who rode her paint-speckled bicycle all over Oberunterdorf. She spoke to us in English sprinkled with German.

"So, Joshua," she said to me. "Today you rest from your long *reise*[1] from America. And tonight I make special schnitzel for you and your sisters, OK?"

That sounded fine to me.

"And tomorrow your Supergranny takes you down to Heidelberg to see the castle," Oma went on.

"Is it true the castle is pink and the French burned it down three times?" Vannie asked.

Oma laughed. "It's pink and burned many times, but it is still big and very beautiful."

Supergranny had just given Baby Sadie back to Oma and we were starting to our rooms to rest when a car roared into the parking lot and squealed to a halt just inches from the guest house wall.

A thin, erect man with a red mustache sprang from a maroon Mercedes. He strode toward the staircase, his heels clicking briskly on the cobblestone courtyard.

"It's Count Otto von Bombast," Oma whispered.

"A count?" Angela asked excitedly. "As in nobility?"

"A real count?" Vannie asked.

Oma's laughing face turned grim. "Indeed, real," she said. "Real *schlecht*."[2]

I remembered *schlecht* from Angela's German phrase book. It meant . . . bad.

---

1. *Reise*. Sound like "rise a." Means "trip."
2. *Schlecht*. Sounds like "shhh leckt." Means "bad."

2

We hit the Porsche early the next morning for the ride
down through the forest to Heidelberg, a very old city
tucked between the hills in the Neckar River Valley.

Picture red tile roofs, brick streets and flowers.

Good.

Now, part way up the hill on the left, picture a giant pink
stone castle. Put in plenty of walls, ramparts, towers and
wings rambling off in all directions.

Very good.

Make some of the walls look crumbled and covered by
vines.

Great.

Be sure to cover the hillside with trees and surround the
castle with dark green leaves.

Perfect.

Now you know what we saw when we clattered across the Old Bridge over the Neckar that morning.

Meanwhile, Angela was blathering on about an English princess who lived in Heidelberg Castle 350 years ago.

Her name was Elizabeth, and Angela had done a report on her. Angela, as you may know, has done a report on everything in the world and gotten *at least* an A- on all of them.

I don't hold that against her, but the problem is when she starts talking about one of those reports, there's no stopping her.

She was going to tell us about Princess Elizabeth or bust, and we knew it. The best thing to do was let her roll on and hope she got it all out of her system before lunch.

"Elizabeth was only sixteen when German Prince Frederick from Heidelberg Castle went to London to meet her. He was dark, handsome and super rich. She was beautiful, with long amber hair and blue eyes, and was also super rich.

"They fell madly in love as soon as he got off the boat. Her father, King James, gave them the biggest wedding the world had ever seen. They both wore white silk and pearls, and the fireworks, banquets, plays and parades went on for days. It cost a fortune, but King James said she was his only daughter, and he was determined to do the wedding up right.

"After the wedding Elizabeth and Frederick crossed the English Channel, then rode across Europe to Heidelberg with 4,000 servants and Elizabeth's pet monkey, Jack."

"Her what?" Vannie asked. The monkey had gotten her attention. Vannie likes monkeys herself and wouldn't mind owning one. Our parents, however, are united against it.

"Her monkey, Jack," Angela repeated. "He rode around on her shoulder and went everywhere with her. He was probably right on her shoulder in 1613 when she first crossed the Neckar River we just crossed."

By then we had wound up, up, up the twisting, narrow brick road to Heidelberg Castle, and Supergranny was parking the Porsche in the castle parking lot.

"Did they live happily ever after in Heidelberg Castle?" Vannie asked as we climbed out of the Porsche.

Angela didn't have time to answer as we passed through the gate to the castle grounds. The first thing we saw was a pink stone archway to our left.

"It's the Elizabeth Gate," Angela said. "There's just grass on the other side now, but 350 years ago it led to a beautiful garden.

"Legend says Frederick loved Elizabeth so much, he had the gate built overnight to surprise her."

"And did they live here happily ever after?" Vannie asked again.

Angela looked solemn.

"For a while. They rode and hunted and entertained and had three beautiful little babies. Dukes and counts and diplomats and minor princesses went out of their way to visit Heidelberg just to say they'd met them.

"They were the Prince Charles and Lady Diana of the 17th century.

"And then . . . " Angela's voice trailed off.

"Then what?" Vannie asked.

"And then," Angela said, " . . . disaster."

Angela didn't go into the disaster right then because we

had to buy our tickets and catch the next guided castle tour.

"It starts in five minutes," Supergranny said, dragging us across the bridge over the moat, then through the gate in the castle wall.

These days the moat doesn't have water in it, but hundreds of years ago it did. The idea was to keep enemies out. When somebody the prince didn't like came galloping up, WHAM, the soldiers dropped the spiked gate in the wall. And there the enemies were — stuck on the wrong side of the moat.

The gate looms over your head like a crocodile's upper teeth, ready to crash on your head, and it made me a tad nervous to walk under it.

But Vannie *Dummkopf*[1] had to stand there staring straight up at the spikes to prove how brave she was.

"Hey, Joshua, look at me," she yelled. "Hey, Angela, look at me."

It was very embarrassing and almost made us late for the tour. We caught up to the guide just as he was leading about ninety tourists into the left wing to look at a scale model of the castle.

He told us about the "Seldom Empty" prison tower (no kidding, it had so many prisoners they called it "Seldom Empty" — only in German, of course). Then he explained about the "Fat Tower" that was partly *kaputt*[2] because the French had managed to roll part of it down the hillside a couple of centuries before.

---

1. *Dummkopf*. Sounds like "doom cope fff." Means "blockhead."
2. *Kaputt*. Sounds like "kuh put." Means "broken."

Then we got to see some of the rooms where the princes and princesses actually lived and held court and all that, starting with the hall of mirrors.

These days the hall of mirrors is fairly bleak with plain stone walls and floors, but in the old days it had been stuffed with gold-framed mirrors, beautiful hanging tapestries to keep out drafts, and all sorts of royalty and nobility dressed in silk and velvet and jewels and wigs.

"Close your eyes," Angela whispered. "And imagine Elizabeth walking through the hall of mirrors with Jack on her shoulder."

I tried, but there were too many people around. And a woman in weird sunglasses and a big head scarf kept bumping me with her camera bag. It spoiled the effect.

My imagination worked better on the castle terrace overlooking the city.

The tour group went on ahead while we stood together in a small tower at one end of the terrace, watching sailboats tack their way around barges on the Neckar below.

Tile roofs, church spires, chimneys, fountains and statues were jumbled together like toys.

"It looks like a city in a story," Vannie said.

"Yes," Supergranny agreed. "This is one of my favorite views in the world. But wait until we come back tonight. It's even better by starlight."

By now the rest of the tour had disappeared, except for the woman in the weird sunglasses and scarf, who was taking pictures like mad.

We caught up in a dark, gloomy, damp cellar where everybody was gawking at a humongous, empty wine barrel. It was big enough to hold a pod of whales, so you can imagine how much wine it held in the old days.

"Cripes, who drank all that wine?" Vannie asked.

"I guess the princes and soldiers and servants and almost everybody else helped," Supergranny said. "No wonder they had so many battles and wars back then. People went around potted two-thirds of the time. Drunks have hair-trigger tempers, you know, not to mention people with hangovers."

"Speaking of wars and battles," Angela said, "that's what happened to Elizabeth and Frederick. The Thirty Years War. It started when . . ."

"Oh, no," I groaned. "You're not going to tell us about a thirty years war?"

"I'll be in college before she finishes," Vannie muttered. "Maybe married."

"Well, it has a lot to do with this castle," Angela said, getting huffy.

Supergranny tried to save us.

"I'm sure it's very interesting, Angela, but it's time we break for lunch. Let's go down into the old town for the best cream-of-chicken soup in Germany."

Angela looked doubtful. When she's wound up to give a report, she'd rather talk than eat.

"It's at the Ritter Hotel," Supergranny said, guiding us out into the sunlight. "It's so old, I wouldn't be surprised if Elizabeth's own kids ate soup there."

That sold Angela.

As for me, I'm not wild about cream-of-chicken soup, but anything beats a thirty years war.

3

It felt good to relax at the Ritter after all the castle sight-seeing that morning.

Our table by the front, round window had fresh flowers, a white tablecloth and napkins, and a good view of people rushing up and down the busy main street outside.

The Ritter also had something else you don't often see in American restaurants.

Dogs.

Yep, dogs. German people take their dogs into restaurants. Over in the corner a very large boxer lay at a woman's feet as she sipped wine. In the middle of the room, a dachshund snoozed under a man's chair.

"I noticed dogs at the Oberunterhof last night," I said, "but I didn't know it was a national custom."

"Oh, yes," Supergranny said. "Germans often take their

dogs into restaurants. And you'll notice they're *very* well behaved."

"Does that mean we can take Shackleford to restaurants with us?" Vannie asked.

We'd left Shackleford and Chesterton in Oberunterdorf to rest up from their jet lag.

"I don't know about Shackleford," Supergranny said. "She's so bashful. I'd hate for her to get startled and turn over a table or something."

Another difference from America was the bread and rolls. They were good, but they were so hard they made our teeth hurt.

"The bread's tough," Vannie said, gnawing on the corner of a roll.

"You'll get used to it," Supergranny said, "Most European bread is like that; Europeans think the soft bread we eat is too mushy."

Just then the waiter brought our cream-of-chicken soup.

"Now, Angela," Supergranny said after we were served, "while we're relaxing can you tell us BRIEFLY what happened to Princess Elizabeth and—"

"Of course," Angela broke in. "Actually—"

"—Just a minute, dear, I'm not finished," Supergranny said. "I mean BRIEFLY. In a three and one? In just three sentences? In only one minute?"

Angela considered.

"Only three sentences?" she asked.

"Yes," Supergranny said.

"Only one minute?" Angela asked.

"You've got it," Supergranny said.

Angela considered some more. 'I'll have to summarize."

13

"By all means," Supergranny said.

"It will be a challenge," Angela said.

"But you like challenges, Angela," Vannie said. "You *always say* you like challenges."

"I think I can do it," Angela said slowly. "When do I start?"

"In thirty seconds," Supergranny said, pulling her stopwatch from her purse. "Joshua, do the countdown and call time."

She handed me the stopwatch and I counted down the seconds: "Ten, nine, eight, seven, six, five, four, three, two, one, go!"

Angela was off. I put the watch on the table beside me and went back to my chicken soup.

She started fast: "Elizabeth and Frederick got tired of being plain old Prince and Princess and decided they wanted to be a King and Queen, so when the old king died in Prague about 400 miles away, they went to Prague and took over the castle, making a lot of other princes mad."

"Twenty seconds," I said, slurping soup.

"So some other princes chased them out of the castle, starting the Thirty Years War, which tore up Europe something awful and caused so much fighting around Heidelberg that Elizabeth and Frederick couldn't get back and had to escape to their rich relatives in Holland where they had ten more children."

"Forty seconds," I said, slurping more soup.

Angela plowed on:

"Then Frederick went back to the war, but didn't see the end of it in 1648 because he got sick on the battlefield and died, leaving Elizabeth a widow in Holland until her nephew, England's King Charles II, invited her back to London where people had forgotten everything about her except that she was Charles' old aunt, BUT, and this is the good part—"

"Ten seconds left," I said.

"—when England ran into king problems, they invited HER GRANDSON to be King George I, making her the greatgreatgreatgreat—"

"One second left," I said.

"—greatgreatgreatgreatgreat grandmother of the present Queen Elizabeth of England!"

"TIME!" I yelled as Angela finished with a flourish, Supergranny hugged her, people at the next three tables clapped and Vannie cheered.

But a man and woman at one nearby table were *not* amused. They turned, scowled at us, shrugged, then went back to whispering intently.

"Don't look now," Vannie said softly, "but isn't that Count von Bombast?"

"Don't look now," I said, "but isn't that woman with him in the scarf and weird sunglasses the same woman who was on our castle tour?"

"Don't look now," Angela said, "but isn't that an *animal* in that basket under her chair? That little basket that looks like a cage?"

The room had become very quiet after Angela's performance. All you could hear were the clinking of glasses, low, murmuring conversation . . . and a strange, shrill chattering.

15

Supergranny shielded her face with her napkin and pretended to pat her mouth. "Something is chattering in that basket," she whispered. "Look when you get the chance. *Casually!*"

Casually, we all glanced toward Count von Bombast's table. He and the woman leaned toward each other, still whispering intently.

The chattering had stopped.

Casually, we all turned back to our soup.

"Did you see it?" Supergranny hissed.

We nodded. We'd all seen it.

A long, hairy, bony finger had poked through the lid of the basket, waved at us, and disappeared.

The weird, bony finger was on our minds all the way back to Oberunterdorf. But we forgot about it when we got to the guest house.

Shackleford and Chesterton were out on the balcony entertaining Oma and Baby Sadie.

Oma was holding Baby Sadie on her lap, and both of them were laughing themselves silly watching Chesterton and Shackleford play "Herd the Robot."

The more they laughed, the more Chesterton and Shackleford hammed it up.

As an Old English sheepdog, Shackleford *loves* to pretend she is herding sheep like her ancestors did for centuries.

She is forever herding us around at home.

Most mornings she is right on my dad's heels while he

gets ready for work. As soon as she barks him out the door, she starts on Angela or Vannie or me or whoever has to be herded off to school next. She always seems to know who's next.

The problem is that if you stop she runs into you, and if you dare turn around, there is a front-on crash.

After we leave for school, she has an hour break before she has to get Mom off to her job at the newspaper. Mom says it's a good thing because Shackleford is so worn out by then she collapses on her back with her legs resting against the front door.

She keeps in form by playing "Herd the Robot" with Chesterton.

It goes like this: Chesterton toodles around with Shackleford right on his rear. Gradually, he picks up speed, then starts ducking under tables and chairs and making sharp turns.

This outfoxes Shackleford for two reasons.

First, because she's about ten times as big as Chesterton she can't fit under all the chairs.

Second, because she can't make sharp turns or sudden stops, she winds up doing acrobatic tricks and crashing into walls.

It's like watching a motor home chase a jeep.

When the game really gets hot and Chesterton makes a sharp turn, Shackleford tries to brake and slides right by, her paws scrambling frantically to try to change directions.

It's funny to watch, but the best part is when Chesterton comes to a dead stop and Shackleford has to jump over him and lands in a somersault.

They pulled that stunt just as we came onto the balcony,

and Shackleford somersaulted right into a flower box of geraniums. Oma laughed so hard Baby Sadie almost slid off her lap; Supergranny grabbed her just in time.

"It looks like they are over their jet lag," Supergranny said drily. "I think we can take them with us to the castle tonight."

*   *   *   *

We spent the afternoon wheeling Baby Sadie around Oberunterdorf in her elegant, dark gray baby buggy, then had terrific wiener schnitzel with the whole family in the guest house's cozy dining room.

So it was already dusk when we got back down to the castle gardens.

"Let's sit down here beside Neptune and write our cards," Supergranny said, sitting beside a fountain of Neptune, Roman god of the sea.

"We have to keep in touch," she said, passing out ball-points and German stamps.

Supergranny is a great believer in Keeping In Touch. In this case that meant sending postcards to our family and friends.

"We've got to get them done tonight and in the mail by tomorrow," she said. "Otherwise, we'll get home before our cards get there. And I despise getting home before my cards do, don't you?"

We agreed that we did, although to tell you the truth, I'd never thought much about it. The only other trip I'd been on without my parents was computer camp, and I couldn't remember if I'd sent cards or not.

Angela, Vannie and I wrote Mom and Dad while Shackleford and Chesterton explored the garden and Supergranny churned out cards to Professor Picklesnip, Office Inspect, Myrtle Witherspoon Richmont,[1] Captain Tubweathers, Clarence,[2] the president, secretary of state, and the New York Giants backfield. Actually, I'm not sure she wrote the last three, but she probably did, because she wrote so many.

"When you travel as much as I do, you learn not to drag it out," she said, polishing off a whole postcard stack before I was past "Dear Mom & Dad . . ."

I was sending them a postcard of the castle in the old days. It was a copy of a painting done by some world famous artist hundreds of years ago. It showed the east garden where we were sitting with the castle in front of us and the Neckar River emptying into the mighty Rhine River way in the distance.

A woman in a long dress was carrying a basket on her head and way down in the corner a man drove an oxcart down a quiet lane.

It looked so peaceful, I could almost picture it in the garden now.

"You'd better hurry with those cards," Supergranny put in, "or it will be too dark to write."

She was right. The setting sun played on the fountain beside us, casting flickering shadows on the stone wall. Old Neptune lay back in the spray, staring past us at the castle tower.

---

1.   See *Supergranny 1: The Mystery of the Shrunken Heads.*
2.   See *Supergranny 2: The Case of the Riverboat Riverbelle.*

The garden was almost deserted.

Without the tourists around and the weird-sunglasses woman bumping me with her camera bag, it was easier to imagine the old days.

"Can't you almost see her?" Angela asked dreamily. "Close your eyes and can't you almost see Princess Elizabeth walking along the garden path? Her long, amber hair is blowing softly in the breeze. Her green, silk gown trails behind her."

I pretended to look down at the postcard I was writing and secretly closed my eyes. I'd never admit it to Angela, but it was true. I *could* see a gorgeous princess in my imagination. I could almost hear her footsteps.

"I can see her," Vannie said excitedly. "Angela, I can see her!"

"Yes, now try to picture Jack the monkey on her shoulder," Angela said in the same dreamy tone.

"I'M NOT IMAGINING!" Vannie yelled. "I CAN SEE HER, look, there on the other side of the garden. FOR PETE'S SAKE, JOSHUA! ANGELA! SUPERGRANNY! OPEN YOUR EYES!"

My eyes sprang open.

There on the other side of the garden was a woman with long, reddish hair. She was wearing a long, green dress. But her hair wasn't blowing gently in the breeze and she wasn't walking softly along the path.

She was running!

She was being chased by a small robot and a large, hairy dog!

5

"CHESTERTON!" Supergranny yelled, jumping up in a scatter of postcards. "CHESTERTON! STOP! *THIS MINUTE!*"

"SHACKLEFORD!" Angela yelled on the run.

"SHACKLEFORD, SHACKLEFORD!" I yelled, chasing after.

"SHACKLEFORD, CHESTERTON, SHACKLEFORD," Vannie yelled, bringing up the rear.

Did that spoiled robot pay the *slightest* attention?

Did that stubborn Old English sheepdog even *pause*? Ha!

On they raced, barking and beeping and trampling flower beds.

The woman, holding her long dress up to her knees, ran like the wind. Her reddish hair streamed behind her.

Shackleford and Chesterton weren't being mean, of course. At least, not on purpose. They must have thought she was playing a game of "Herd the Robot" with them.

I could just picture their little brain and microchip going, "Oboy!" "New Game With Woman Who Looks Like Long-Dead English Princess!" "Fun!" "Run!" "Fun!" "Run!"

Which doesn't excuse them one *pfennig*[1] in my book.

The woman didn't know they were playing. Probably no one else in Germany would believe they were playing.

I could just see us getting thrown out of Germany in disgrace for bringing an attack robot and dog to Heidelberg Castle. Or thrown into the Seldom Empty Prison Tower.

The woman rounded the far corner and started cutting across flower beds, jumping over flowers and small shrubs as she went.

Shackleford missed the turn, her paws scrambling frantically on the path trying to get enough traction to change direction.

Chesterton, who can make a 90-degree turn faster than you can flip a light switch, whipped after her, flashing and beeping and pretending to grab the hem of her dress.

By now Supergranny was getting winded and ready to resort to bribery.

"GUMDROPS, CHESTERTON, GUMDROPS," she shouted.

Chesterton, as you may know, is fueled by gumdrops that you pop into a coffee cup-shaped sensor on top his head. He loves and adores them and would gobble them by the box-car load if you let him. Sometimes when he

---

1. *Pfennig.* Sounds like "fen ig." Means a German coin worth less than one penny.

23

goes hyper and runs off, Supergranny bribes him to stop with gumdrops.

If you think that spoils him worse, I'm with you. But there's no point trying to tell Supergranny. She considers him her robot and her business.

Anyway, this time even gumdrops didn't work. For one thing, he was making so much noise he probably didn't hear her.

By now Angela had caught up to Shackleford. She was preaching a "Naughty Dog" sermon as the rest of us sailed past. We caught up to Chesterton sniffing around an old wooden door in the garden wall.

Supergranny scooped him up, launching into a Triple Deluxe tongue lashing. I'd never seen her so steamed at Chesterton.

"AND THE NEXT TIME YOU'LL STAY HOME IN AMERICA WITH A BABYSITTER, BLAH, BLAH, BLAH," she yelled.

"OR AT A ROBOT KENNEL IF THIS IS THE WAY YOU'RE GOING TO ACT, BLAH, BLAH, BLAH.

"WE'RE ALL TRYING TO BE POLITE GUESTS IN ANOTHER COUNTRY AND YOU — BLAH, BLAH, BLAH.

"YOU'LL SPEND THE REST OF THIS TRIP IN VAN-NIE'S BACKPACK IF YOU DON'T STRAIGHTEN UP!!!"

She really gave it to him, and I'm sorry to admit that I enjoyed it. I like Chesterton, but you wouldn't *believe* what he gets away with sometimes.

He turned off his lights and beeper and tried to look innocent, but it didn't work.

"DON'T YOU DARE TRY TO LOOK INNOCENT WITH

ME!" Supergranny barked. "DON'T YOU DARE!"

By then, Angela came up with an embarrassed Shackleford on the leash.

"Where is she?" Angela asked.

We looked around blankly. We'd been so caught up in Supergranny's tirade we'd forgotten about the mysterious woman.

The shadowy garden was empty.

"She's gone," Vannie whispered.

"But where?" Angela asked slowly.

Supergranny tried the heavy wooden door in the garden wall.

"Locked," she said.

"Hello?" Angela called, knocking briskly. "Are you in there? Are you all right?"

Silence.

She knocked again.

Again, silence.

We were alone in the garden.

The woman had disappeared.

*   *   *   *

An hour later we sat on the castle terrace with Shackleford and Chesterton huddled under our bench in disgrace.

The lights of the old city sparkled below us. Around us, the castle walls were bathed in honey-colored floodlights. Tourists from around the world strolled past, babbling a dozen languages.

But we could talk of only one thing: the mysterious woman in the garden.

Who was she? Why did she wear such strange clothes? Where had she come from? Where had she gone?

"She was right in front of me, not thirty feet away with Chesterton on her heels," Supergranny said. "They both ran behind a tree and three seconds later when I caught up — poof — she was gone. There was Chesterton alone, sniffing around the garden wall."

"Could she have climbed over the wall?" Vannie asked.

"In three seconds? A ten-foot wall? Wearing a long dress? Get real, Vannie," I said.

After we had finished balling out Shackleford and Chesterton, we had searched that section of the garden on the off chance the poor woman had tripped or fallen under a bush or something.

No woman.

Then we reported the incident at the castle office. It had taken some doing, but Supergranny finally talked one of the castle guards into coming back to the garden with us.

He was a little frosty at first, but Supergranny managed to get him to unlock the heavy wooden door in the garden wall in case the woman had dashed in there to hide from Chesterton and gotten locked in by mistake.

It turned out to be a dark, dank storage room. Supergranny whipped out her heavy duty flashlight, and we went over every inch of it with the guard's help.

No woman.

Nothing but garden tools, bags of manure and some three-hundred-year-old cobwebs and smells.

By now the guard, Herr Hinkel, had thawed out a bit, and he and Supergranny were chattering away in German. All I could pick up was *"Gut, gut,"*[1] which meant "Good, good," and *"Danke, danke,"*[2] which meant "Thanks, thanks."

But there had been more, as Supergranny explained later. For one thing, we weren't the first to have seen a mysterious young woman in the castle garden.

"He said some Japanese tourists spotted her at dusk last night," Supergranny said. "They thought perhaps she was dressed up for a play or pageant. They went to the castle office and asked what time the play started.

"But there wasn't any play.

"And the night before, two honeymooners from Paw Paw, West Virginia, heard a woman crying by the Neptune fountain. But when they got to the statue, nobody was there."

"I just wish we could apologize to her for Shackleford and Chesterton," Vannie said. "And I wish we could be sure she was all right."

"She's all right," Angela whispered.

We stared at her. How did she know the woman was all right?

Angela was gazing above our heads at an upper window in the castle's Friedrich's Wing. We turned to look. A hush fell over the babble of voices around us as everyone on the terrace turned to stare.

The woman stood at the castle window looking down on Heidelberg. She was beautiful, silent, unsmiling.

---

1. *Gut.* Sounds like "goot." Means good.
2. *Danke.* Sounds like "Don keh." Means thank you.

Supergranny whipped her binoculars out of her purse, took a quick look, and passed them around.

A small monkey sat on the woman's shoulder, his long, bony fingers twirling strands of her beautiful amber hair.

Suddenly, the woman began to scream. The terrible, maddening sound of her scream flooded the night air.

Then, in front of our eyes, the woman and the monkey began to dissolve . . . and disappeared.

6

Things happened fast after that.

For a few seconds, everyone on the terrace froze. Then the babble of languages broke out again, faster and noisier than ever.

Pick a language, any language, and I guarantee you somebody was shouting it on that terrace: German, Japanese, French, Spanish, English, Italian, Hindi, Norwegian, Kurdish, Turkish, Chinese, the works.

And nobody was listening in any language.

Suddenly, in the midst of all this, a man staggered beneath the castle archway onto the terrace.

"Geist, geist,"[1] he said hoarsely, then collapsed in front of us. He was thin, trim and had a red mustache.

---

1.   *Geist.* Rhymes with "heist." Means ghost.

"Count Otto von Bombast," Supergranny said, springing to his side.

"Code Seven," she said calmly as she picked up his wrist to count his pulse.

"Code Seven" means come close, keep calm, and follow orders.

She gave us our orders:

"Vannie, cover him with our jackets. His pulse is racing and he could go into shock.

"Angela, find a guard to call an ambulance.

"Joshua, take Shackleford and the flashlight and get up to that castle window. One floor down from the top, fourth window from the corner. Find out what the heck is going on.

"Chesterton, stay UNDER that bench and OUT of trouble."

I grabbed the flashlight and Shackleford's leash and dashed for the stairway in the castle courtyard. Angela ran beside me to find a guard.

Adding to the pandemonium, someone had turned off the floodlights. The castle was in darkness.

Angela and I parted in the courtyard.

"Bombast said 'geist,'" she shouted over her shoulder. "It means 'ghost.' 'Geist' is German for 'ghost.'"

I ran up the outer stairway and pushed my way through a heavy door into a dark hallway. This part of the castle was off limits to tourists, and it was as quiet as a tomb. My flashlight beam danced eerily on the stone walls.

Footsteps clattered upstairs, one floor above.

I took a deep breath and started up the steps with Shackleford bounding ahead, pulling me along on the leash.

She seemed happy to be back in action after being banished under the bench in disgrace. And, frankly, I was happy to have her.

I figured the whatever-it-was-in-the-long-dress had run from Shackleford once. And if we rounded a corner and ran smack into the whatever-it-was-in-the-long-dress, I would just as soon it ran in the other direction again.

You'll notice I wasn't letting myself think the word "g---t."

For one thing, I don't believe in "g---ts." Most of the time.

For another, "g---t" is an OK word to use when you're guzzling pop and gulping pizza at a party, or spending the night with a friend, or telling strange stories to cousins and other people.

But it's not so OK when you're by yourself at night in a dark, cold, 400-year-old castle. Especially when you've just watched a mysterious screaming woman disappear in front of your eyes *twice* in the last hour.

It's amazing how much you don't want to think "g---t" at times like that.

So I tried not to think it as Shackleford and I dashed up the stairs.

When we'd run up what must have been at least 736 steps, we came to a hallway with lots of clattering and shouting going on down at the other end.

I stopped on the top step, reined in Shackleford, and switched off the flashlight. Quietly, I leaned around the corner to check out the noise.

Several shadowy figures were down at the other end, banging on a door and shouting in German. They were carrying flashlights and wearing uniforms.

Obviously, they were castle guards on the same mission I was: to find out what the heck the mysterious woman was doing in the castle window.

Obviously, they'd figured out which room she had been in.

"Shhhh, Shackleford," I whispered. "Be very quiet."

Shackleford and I tiptoed down the hall, then lurked in the shadows about six feet from the commotion.

One of the guards was fiddling with a large brass ring of keys. He looked like the guard who'd gone with us to the garden, but I couldn't be sure in the darkness.

He was trying one key after the other, but he kept getting them upside down and losing his place. I think the other guards were making him nervous by shouting and shining their flashlights in his eyes.

At last the lock clicked, kicking off much excitement and even louder shouting on the part of the other guards. He pushed down the door lever, but, try as he might, the door wouldn't budge.

He pushed again.

Nothing happened.

The other three couldn't stand it. They all leaned over him and pushed against the door. Slowly, it creaked open, stirring a flurry of dust that made both Shackleford and me sneeze.

Luckily, the guards were so excited, they didn't hear us.

They bounded into the room, nearly tripping each other in their haste.

Shackleford and I slipped in after them.

Four flashlight beams played around the room. With all that light I figured we didn't need mine, so I kept it in my pocket.

Their light danced around the walls and in the corners.

But there was no princess, no monkey and no ghost — at least, not one that you could see.

All that showed up were thick cobwebs, bunches of old furniture covered with blankets, Shackleford and me.

Whatever the guards had expected to find, it wasn't us, and it made them mad.

They took turns yelling at us in German while they whipped blankets off the furniture, checking for hiding princesses. I couldn't understand what they were yelling, but I was pretty sure it was along the line, "GET OUT, OR WE'LL THROW YOU IN PRISON."

I grinned, nodded and blabbered that I couldn't speak German while I dragged Shackleford to the window and looked out.

The room was one floor down from the top.

The window was fourth from the corner.

It was the right room.

But it was empty.

And from the look of it, it had been empty for a long, long time.

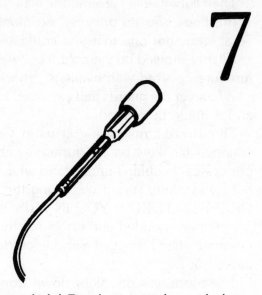

7

The emergency squad slid Bombast into the ambulance just as I got back to the courtyard.

"To the Porsche!" Supergranny yelled. We all raced to the parking lot, jumped into the Porsche and headed for the hospital.

We got there as Bombast was wheeled through the emergency room's double doors still muttering *"Geist, geist."*[1]

The hospital staff X-rayed his head and kept him for observation for about an hour.

Meanwhile, the tourists who had watched the whole thing from the castle terrace flowed down into town bursting with news about Heidelberg Castle's vanishing woman and collapsing count.

---

1. *Geist.* Rhymes with "heist." Means ghost.

First, they spread the news through every restaurant and cafe in Heidelberg. Then they got on the phone to their parents, aunts, uncles, friends, cousins and former roommates throughout Germany, Japan, Spain, England, America, Italy, India, Norway, the Middle East, Turkey, China and France.

Pretty soon, the press got wind of it. By the time the doctors figured out that the count wasn't even scratched, their waiting room was packed with press people, and Bombast was making a statement — in English, German and French. (He didn't want *any* reporter to miss this.)

"I have met the ghost of an English princess," he announced grandly.

At that, some reporters ooooed, some ahhhed, and some giggled.

"But I am too overcome to talk tonight," Bombast went on.

"However, ladies and gentlemen of the international press are invited to the Oberunterhof guest house tomorrow morning at 10 for a press conference."

With that, he strode toward the hospital steps where he turned with a flourish.

"At that time I will reveal the secret of the ghost of Heidelberg Castle."

*　　　*　　　*　　　*

Reporters and camera crews began pouring into the village early the next morning. By 9:30 a.m., the guest house was a madhouse. Television light cords crisscrossed the dining room, and the line to use the telephone stretched out the door, down the steps and all the way to the butcher shop.

Rolf and Meg ran around like crazy people, setting up tables, chairs and microphones and keeping the coffee cups washed and filled.

Meanwhile, Oma served fruit tortes and *schnecken*[1] (sweet rolls shaped like snails) by the hundreds. She had used up all she baked by 9:45 a.m., and Vannie and I had to run to the bakery three times for more.

"All this is good for business," Rolf said, pushing me out the door to the bakery again. "But I wish we'd had more notice."

"It's exciting that people all over the world will see the Oberunterhof on TV," Meg said. "But I wish it weren't because of the count. I don't trust him. If you ask me, he's slipperier than soap."

"It's fun," Oma said. "But I wish I'd baked more tortes."

Angela cleared tables, and Supergranny was put in complete charge of Baby Sadie, which thrilled her down to her stars-and-stripes tennis shoes.

"It's about time," she whispered. "I've been trying to get the baby all to myself ever since I landed. But I never thought I'd be helped by Princess Elizabeth."

Because that's what the press conference was all about, of course. Bombast was gearing up to tell the world how he had met the ghost of Princess Elizabeth of Heidelberg Castle.

When Vannie and I got back from our third bakery run, the press conference was just getting rolling.

---

1. *Schnecken.* Sounds like "shh neckin'." Means snails. In this case, snail-shaped pastries.

We dropped the schnecken and tortes in the kitchen, then slid into the seats Angela and Supergranny had saved for us in the last row.

Supergranny was bouncing Baby Sadie on her knee, singing softly and tut-tut-tutting.

Bombast marched into the room at the last minute, his heels clicking briskly on the polished hardwood floor.

He was all business.

"Ladies and gentlemen," he said, after tapping the mike and saying "Testing, one, two, three," a couple of times. "Thank you for coming this morning to hear about the strange events of the evening past.

"There will be doubters among you, I am sure. Skeptics will say I did not hear what I heard, did not see what I saw.

"So be it.

"But I remind you that it is not just I, Bombast, an ordinary count, a simple nobleman, who witnessed this amazing sight.

"Dozens, nay, hundreds, of people from around the world saw the strange spirit at Heidelberg Castle last evening.

"So those who doubt me, the humble Bombast, also doubt witnesses from around the world. Witnesses who were as shocked, as stunned, as surprised as I by the events of the past evening.

"However, there is no need to waste your time and mine.

"Ladies and gentlemen, those of you who don't believe that I, Bombast, and hundreds of witnesses saw the ghost of Princess Elizabeth of Heidelberg Castle . . . I invite you to leave.

37

"In fact, I insist.

"NOW!" he shouted sharply, causing Baby Sadie to jump. She wrinkled her face to cry, but Supergranny hugged her and restarted "tut-tut-tutting" to settle her down.

Of course, he had the reporters over a barrel.

They couldn't leave without SOME kind of a story, so they had to stay. Staying didn't mean they believed he'd met a ghost any more than they believed he was premier of France. But they had to stay.

Some of the reporters shifted uneasily in their chairs, some laughed, and some muttered "baaaaaaloney."

But nobody left.

"Sooooo," Bombast said grandly. "We understand each other.

"Now, pay careful attention, my friends.

"Last night the ghost of the beautiful English Princess Elizabeth, daughter of King James I of England, wife of the German Prince Frederick V, appeared to me in the courtyard of Heidelberg Castle."

"Did she say anything?" a woman reporter asked.

Almost everybody laughed.

Bombast didn't seem to mind. He smiled, in fact. Slyly.

The laughter died.

"Oh, yes, dear lady, indeed she did. A great deal."

"What did she say?" asked a man by the window.

"She said she couldn't rest as long as she and her dear Frederick — that's what she call him, 'my dear Frederick' — were still being blamed for starting the Thirty Years War.

"'It wasn't our fault,' she said. She said that over and over. 'It wasn't our fault.'

"And she said those stories about Frederick running away from a battle and losing his garter were rubbish. Totally false. She's *very* angry about that."

"Not to change the subject," Supergranny said. "But why did you collapse on the castle terrace last night? I mean, other than to attract the attention of the entire world? Apparently, you hadn't been hurt."

He smiled that sly smile again.

"I was overcome, dear lady. Overwhelmed. I'd never talked to a ghost before."

"Did the princess say anything else?" asked a French reporter in the back row with us.

"She didn't say anything else..." Bombast said.

A few reporters started to get up to leave.

"... but she gave me something."

The reporters sat back down.

"She entrusted me with her own, original diary written from 1613 to 1648. A never-before-seen account of the early 17th century written in her own hand. The food they ate, the clothes they wore, jokes, sports, festivals, politics and, of course, the Thirty Years War.

"It's going to blow the lid off 17th-century European history. They'll rewrite the history books after this."

"Where is the diary?" asked the man by the window.

"Where is the diary?" asked the French reporter.

"The Elizabeth Diary is in a well-guarded hiding place," Bombast said. "I alone know its whereabouts."

"And what are you going to do with it?" Supergranny asked.

"Bombast's sly smile broke into a broad grin and then into a haunting laugh.

"I'm going to sell it, dear heart.

"The Elizabeth Diary is for sale. At this very minute my office is contacting major publishers in Europe and America. We will accept sealed bids beginning tomorrow."

"How much?" asked the French reporter.

"Bidding starts at one million dollars," boomed Bombast. "Film rights are extra, of course."

8

The village of Oberunterdorf curves in layers around a small valley, and each layer is threaded with paths.

That afternoon Oma took baby Sadie and the rest of us for a walk around the village while Meg and Rolf tried to put the guest house back together after the press conference uproar.

We took turns pushing Baby Sadie's elegant, dark gray buggy and stopped first at *Esel Ecke*[1] (Donkey Corner) to see Farmer Schwarz's donkeys.

Like many Oberunterdorfers, Farmer Schwarz had a stable attached to his house. But his three donkeys spent most of their time in a small pasture shaped like a triangle.

---

1. *Esel*. Rhymes with Hazel. Means donkey.
   Ecke. Sounds like "Ek Ah." Means corner.

Two roads running alongside met at one of the triangle's points.

Oberunterdorfers used "Esel Ecke" as a landmark and often gave directions by saying, "My house is the third house on the right after Esel Ecke," or "Turn left at Esel Ecke" and so on.

Oma explained all this as we patted the donkeys and tried to keep Chesterton from running under the fence and causing a donkey stampede.

From Esel Ecke we took a path through the woods and came out in a pasture above the chicken farm.

Supergranny and Oma sat down on a bench, and the rest of us plopped down on the ground beside them. It felt good to stretch out in the sunshine and enjoy the view.

And it was some view.

Tile-roofed houses with fenced flower gardens rimmed the valley. Far below, members of the Oberunterdorf riding club, wearing red coats and breeches, jumped a stream and cantered into the woods. Sheep grazed in the pasture, and hens clucked busily in the chicken farm's barnyard.

It was some view, all right, and it took our minds clear off ghosts — for at least thirty seconds.

"Charming view," Supergranny said. "Absolutely charming, but we've got to get to work. Vannie, hand me my clipboard."

Supergranny had wedged her clipboard beneath the side brace on Baby Sadie's buggy, tying it with the special grosgrain ribbon she carries everywhere.

She pulled a pen out of her purse while Vannie untied the clipboard.

"OK, let's review," she said. "Angela, please start by reviewing the problem."

Angela looked out over the valley while she organized her thoughts. So did Vannie and I, because we knew we were next. We couldn't just sit there and daydream. We had to be ready.

"The problem is that Count Bombast may be pulling a humongous fraud," she said slowly.

"Agreed," Supergranny said. "Joshua?"

"Bombast may be trying to convince the world he met Princess Elizabeth's ghost so he can sell her phony diary for a million dollars," I said.

"Agreed," Supergranny said. "Vannie?"

"We have to find out how he's doing it and stop him," Vannie said.

"Right," Supergranny said. "Do we all agree?"

We all nodded that we agreed. Or at least Oma, Angela, Vannie and I nodded. Baby Sadie was asleep, and Shackleford and Chesterton were staring at the barnyard, wishing they could start a game of "Herd the Chickens." Don't ask me how I knew. Somehow, I just knew.

"Good, we agree," Supergranny said. "Now Oma, the day we arrived you let us know you distrust Bombast. You called him *schlecht*[1] or bad."

"And today Meg called him slipperier than soap," I put in.

"But why?" Supergranny asked. "Why don't you trust Bombast?"

"Many reasons," Oma answered, absently pushing Baby Sadie's buggy back and forth.

---

1. *Schlecht.* Sounds like "shhh leckt." Means "bad."

"I first heard of Bombast years ago when Rolf was just a baby. I had a long illness and went with Rolf to stay with my aunt near Frankfurt.

"My aunt knew about this man, this Bombast. He was young then, not long out of university. But already he was known as a cheat and scoundrel.

"I did not meet him then, but my aunt knew him. She cleaned houses for people in Frankfurt, and one of her employers was an elderly professor. He was a kindly old bachelor, good to her, and she was fond of him.

"One day this Bombast came around. He was the professor's cousin or something; I don't remember. He had some papers that he claimed proved the old man's money really belonged to Bombast. And the house, too — everything.

"Bombast came every day with lawyers and more papers. Every day, more lawyers, more papers, more yelling.

"My aunt tried to get the old man to stand up to Bombast, to hire a lawyer himself, but he was old and ill and had no stomach for fighting. Finally, he gave in and signed the papers. Bombast got everything, and the professor had to move to a rest home. My aunt went to see him, but he was very sad and soon he died. My aunt was so angry; she blamed Bombast."

"No wonder you distrust him," Angela said.

"And there are other things," Oma went on. "The first time he stayed at the guest house he tried to leave without paying. When Rolf stopped him he pretended that he had already paid, then that he had just forgotten. And always he makes such a fuss when we clean his bathroom."

44

"Bathroom?" Vannie asked.

"Yes. Once when I went in to clean his bathroom at the guest house, there was black paper taped over the windows. Very strange. I took it down, of course, and he had a fit. He raved. Never have we had a guest rave like that. So now we must always leave the black paper over the window. Believe me, he is a strange man."

"Black paper," Supergranny muttered. "I see ... I think I'm beginning to understand."

At the time I didn't have the foggiest idea what black paper taped to a bathroom window had to do with a Heidelberg Castle ghost. Supergranny said we'd get back to it later.

"Right now I have a question for Angela," she said. "What's this garter business Bombast mentioned at the press conference? Did Frederick lose a garter?"

Angela nodded. "He might have. King James in England took Frederick into the famous 'Order of the Garter' in London. The members always get a fancy garter. It's supposed to be a real honor.

"Later, during the Thirty Years War, Frederick's enemies claimed they found the garter in a captured baggage wagon. After that cartoons all over Europe lampooned Frederick as the prince who ran away and lost his garter."

"That must have been embarrassing," Vannie said.

"It was," Angela said. "But what was a little embarrassment when people were being killed off left and right, crops were being destroyed, and whole towns burned? You'd think they would have shrugged it off. But it was a big deal at the time, and Frederick's friends spent a lot of time denying the story.

"Now I have a question for you, Supergranny," Angela said. "Last night you said Bombast's pulse was racing and he might be going into shock. Wouldn't somebody who had just seen a ghost be likely to go into shock?"

Supergranny laughed. "Probably, but I was mistaken last night. Bombast's pulse raced, then quickly returned to normal.

"He could have faked the increase by running in place before coming out to the terrace. Or maybe just running from the courtyard to the terrace was enough to drive it up. At any rate, it was back to normal eons before the ambulance came. I'm almost sure he faked that collapse, fast pulse rate and all."

She glanced at her watch. "We've got to get back to the guest house. Let's summarize."

She ripped an outline from the clipboard and held it up. It went like this:

The Case of the Heidelberg Castle Ghost

I. Bombast
   A. Swindled old professor
   B. Left Oberunterhof without paying
   C. Appears arrogant and greedy
   D. Taped black paper over bathroom windows

E. Was seen at the Ritter with a mysterious woman carrying a mysterious basket holding a mysterious chattering critter with a long, bony finger

F. Probably faked collapse on castle terrace

G. Will get $1 million if he can convince the world Heidelberg Castle is haunted

II. Ghost

A. Woman who looked like Princess Elizabeth seen in the castle garden

B. Chased by Shackleford and Chesterton

C. Disappeared

D. Seen again in a castle window

E. Disappeared

F. Room where she was seen was locked and empty, with no trace of human entry

G. Identified by Bombast as Princess Elizabeth; reported to have given him her diary

The upshot was we were 98 percent sure we didn't believe in the ghost and 100 percent sure we didn't believe Bombast.

The problem was we'd seen the ghost. With our own eyes. Twice.

10

"Phone, Aunt Sadie. Long distance. Frankfurt," Meg called from the balcony as we crossed the road to the Oberunterhof.

She was talking to Supergranny, of course. Since Supergranny is Meg's aunt, she always calls her "Aunt Sadie."

Supergranny took the call at Meg's desk in the empty Oberunterhof dining room. We all gathered around to find out who was calling from Frankfurt.

It was Cousin Carl, our copilot.

He had heard Bombast's press conference on the radio and wanted to know if that was really Supergranny's voice he'd heard asking questions.

He wanted to know a million other things, too: Had we met Bombast? Was he staying at The Oberunterhof? Had we seen the ghost? Was it a *real* ghost? Did we know where the diary was? And on and on.

"Yes, Carl. Yes, Carl. Yes, Carl. Yes, Carl, No, Carl. No, Carl," Supergranny answered.

Finally, he must have run out of questions because the "Yes-Carl-No-Carl-Yes-Carls" stopped, and she began listening intently.

"You don't say," she said.

"Embezzlement?

"And when was she released?

"And you're sure about the red hair?"

By now, Angela, Vannie and I were itching to know what was going on.

We tried jumping on one foot, sticking our faces in front of Supergranny and mouthing, "Embezzlement??? Who???"

Then Vannie tried the old write-it-on-a-notepad-and-wave-it-in-front-of-person-on-phone trick.

"Who??? What's up???" she scribbled on a Oberunterhof envelope and waved it in front of Supergranny's nose.

Supergranny frowned, turned her back on us and kept right on going as if we weren't there.

We thought the conversation was winding down when she got to the "Yes, we're having a lovely time, too" and "Haven't we been lucky about the weather" stage.

But then she asked, "How's Waltrop?" and he was off again.

The suspense was torture, but finally she got back to what a lovely time everybody was having and, at last, signed off.

"Whew!" she said. "Waltrop's family doesn't speak

English, so Carl hadn't spoken English in two days. Two days of English words were dammed up inside him; I think he was ready to burst.

"Anyway, here's the scoop..."

She paused and glanced around the dining room. Oma had left to put Baby Sadie to bed; we could hear Meg and Rolf clattering around the kitchen.

The dining room was empty.

"Come closer," she whispered. "I don't want Bombast to walk in and hear this."

We gathered as close as we could.

"Waltrop's sister knows the Bombasts," she whispered. "She works in a butcher shop where they buy their meat.

"It seems Bombast has a younger sister, who used to work in a large Frankfurt bank. She went to jail five years ago for embezzling money from the bank.

"Last week she was released."

"Does Carl know what she looks like?" I asked.

"Late twenties," Supergranny whispered. "Quite pretty with long, red hair."

*   *   *   *

"Is it still there?" Angela asked, carrying a supper tray into Supergranny's room.

"Yep," I answered, my binoculars trained on Bombast's maroon Mercedes.

Vannie followed Angela with another tray. She balanced on one foot and kicked the door closed behind her with the other. We couldn't take a chance on Bombast hearing us.

We were eating supper in Supergranny's room, where we had camped since Carl's call.

"Plan 227B," Supergranny had ordered, as soon as she'd finished telling us about Bombast's embezzling sister.

Plan 227B meant "Tail Bombast."

"Maybe he'll lead us to the diary," Supergranny said.

"Or maybe we'll find out how he did the ghost," Angela said.

"Or maybe we'll find the ghost," Vannie said.

We stared at her.

Did Vannie believe the ghost was real?

"I mean the pretend ghost," Vannie said quickly. "Or whatever."

The truth is, it was hard not to slide into thinking, well, maybe there is a ghost, who knows? Who can say for sure? I mean, just because Bombast is a jerk, that doesn't *necessarily* mean he hadn't met something — well — strange.

I decided it was best not to mention that line of thought to the others. Besides, we had to get started on 227B.

The trouble with 227B is that it can get pretty boring.

This time it started off all right. Supergranny gassed up the Porsche, then parked it by the nearest guest house back door, so we could make a quick exit if Bombast left.

Then I had to feed Shackleford and Chesterton and coax them into the waiting Porsche while Vannie and Angela gathered up the jackets, binoculars, flashlights and other stuff we might need.

But all that seemed hours ago. Since then we'd sat around, taking turns doing 20-minute stints at the window while the others just lounged around.

Supergranny tried to get us to nap.

"Who knows how late we'll be up?" she said. "Maybe all night."

But nobody was in the mood to sleep. Angela quizzed us with German words in her phrase book until we all got sick of that and just sat around.

It was a relief to finish my shift and turn the binoculars over to Vannie. I attacked the soup, fruit, bread and cheese on the trays. Not that I was hungry, but at least eating was something to do.

After supper we played rummy for a while and later, I don't know when, I finally dozed off in a chair.

When I awoke the room was dark.

"Hurry," Supergranny hissed from the window. "Bombast is heading for the Mercedes."

I heard a car door slam.

We raced from the room, clattered down the stairs and jumped into the Porsche, scaring the wazootsies out of Chesterton and Shackleford.

11

The Mercedes turned onto the Heidelberg road as we rounded the guest house corner.

"We'll stay one curve behind," Supergranny said. "No sense advertising that we're behind him."

The twisting, narrow road down through the Odenwald forest was dark and deserted. Tall fir trees surrounded us. Many had lost their lower branches, and faint moonlight glowed around their straight, stark trunks.

"It looks like rooms," Vannie whispered. "Rooms of moonlight in the clearings."

The only sounds were the call of an owl following us through the forest and the faint catch of the Mercedes' brakes on the curves ahead.

Was Bombast going to meet the ghost? Was he going after the diary?

"Keep your eyes on that red taillight," Supergranny said. "There are no roads for him to turn off until we reach the valley, but there are plenty of parking spots leading to footpaths. It would be easy to miss him if he pulled into one of those."

I hoped with all my heart he wouldn't. The night was spooky enough without getting out of the Porsche to follow a man through a dark forest to meet a ghost.

"Keep moving, Bombast," I muttered to myself. "Don't stop now."

"Whoops," Supergranny said. "I forgot about the straight stretch beside the meadow."

We'd rounded the bend to the one long stretch of road halfway down the hill, and Bombast's Mercedes was smack ahead of us. Supergranny slowed the Porsche until he reached the end of the straight stretch and rounded the next curve.

Had he seen us?

The owl flapped across the meadow on our left and fluttered to rest in a distant pine.

"I wish that darned owl would turn around and go back to Oberunterdorf," Angela said crossly. "It's giving me the willies."

"Yeah, owl," Vannie said. "Go home and eat mice."

"Don't make it mad," I said, half-joking. I say "half joking" because although I know lots of people love owls, personally, they give me the creeps.

Supergranny, who happens to be an owl lover, laughed. "Shame on you. The poor owl likes us and wants to come along, and you talk about him like that."

It seemed to be taking forever to get to the valley.

"I don't remember this road being so long yesterday," Angela said. "I think it's been stretched."

"We're almost to the bottom," Supergranny said. "And I think I know where he's going."

So did I. Once again, we clattered across the Old Bridge over the Neckar River. Once again, we wound up the steep, brick road to the Heidelberg Castle parking lot.

Supergranny stopped the Porsche in the shadows while Bombast parked, then slipped in beside a large van three spots away.

"Leash Shackleford and bag Chesterton," she said. Vannie quickly snapped on Shackleford's leash while Angela stuffed Chesterton in her tote.

We climbed out of the Porsche and peered around the back of the van.

Bombast's heels clicked across the bricks to the entrance.

"What's he carrying?" Angela whispered.

"Suitcases," Vannie answered.

Each hand gripped two large cases. They must have been heavy, because halfway to the entrance he set them down for a minute to rest.

What was inside?

"Whatever it is," said Angela, "it's too big for a diary."

"And too small for an English princess," said Vannie.

"And just the right size," said Supergranny, "for making a ghost."

12

We almost lost Bombast in the castle courtyard.

It was intermission of "The Student Prince," a very popular play about a prince who falls in love with a Heidelberg barmaid. It was being presented in the courtyard, and the place was packed.

"Drat," Supergranny said. "I didn't count on 137,000 people in the courtyard."

Just then, Angela spotted him.

"Look! There under the arch. He's talking to someone."

We were off, racing around moving walls of people and getting separated in the crowd. Shackleford and I got to the arch first, just as someone disappeared into the doorway I'd gone in before — the door that led to *the* room one floor from the top, fourth window from the corner. Another figure disappeared through the arch to the terrace.

Supergranny and the others fought through the last thicket of playgoers, and I briefed them on what I'd seen.

"Plan 432B," Supergranny barked. "Does everyone have whistles?"

We nodded.

"Angela, Joshua and Shackleford, take the door into the castle. Vannie, Chesterton and I will take the terrace."

Angela, Shackleford and I slipped up the outer stairs and through the doorway, and Angela quietly pulled the heavy door closed behind us.

The castle was darker than night in the Odenwald. No moonlit clearing here. Just darkness, more darkness, and beyond that, darkness.

We squeezed our eyes shut for a minute to help them adjust. Standing with my eyes shut I listened for footsteps, but could hear only the orchestra tuning up for the second act of "Student Prince."

I opened my eyes. Now at least I could see the outline of the stone steps and railing.

I pointed up, and Angela grasped the railing and started slowly up the stairs.

I started to follow with Shackleford, but she wouldn't budge.

The night before, she had practically dragged me up those same stairs. What was wrong with her now?

Whatever it was, she wouldn't budge. She gripped the floor with all four paws and gave me her stubborn look.

I pulled the leash. She gripped the floor harder, her back paws sliding up against her front paws and the collar pushing the hair on her neck up around her ears.

Meanwhile, Angela, not paying the slightest attention,

forged ahead without us.

"Angela, wait," I whispered. On she went, disappearing into the darkness.

The first rule of Plan 432B is "Stick Together," and I was so mad at both of them I could have spit. I wanted to yell, "FOR PETE'S SAKE, ANGELA, HANG ON UNTIL I CAN MOVE THIS DUMMKOPF[1] DOG," but "Silence" is the second 432B rule, so I didn't.

Finally, I more or less dragged the most stubborn dog in history up the steps as she whined and coughed and made more noise than a clothes dryer tumbling coffee pots.

After what seemed like several months we came to the same hallway we'd found before — one floor down from the top. At least, I thought it was the same. By my count it was the same.

I stopped and pulled Shackleford close to me. She was trembling. I scratched her behind the ear and tried to figure out what to do next. Where was Angela? Why was Shackleford trembling? Should I go back for Supergranny?

Suddenly, the hallway began to glow.

Shackleford pressed against my legs, trembling harder.

Nothing happened.

The hallway kept glowing. Nothing kept happening.

The light seemed to be coming from the end of the hall with *the* room. Obviously, I had to lean around the corner and look down the hall.

I counted to ten while I worked up my courage.

Now or never, I thought. Slowly, I leaned around the corner and looked down the hall.

_____

1.   *Dummkopf.* Sounds like "doom cope fff." Means "blockhead."

Everything had changed.

The hallway glowed in the light of a dozen candles. Gold-framed mirrors and tapestries hung on the wall.

The woman stood at a small table. She wore a long green dress and reddish hair fell around her shoulders. A monkey clambered around the table, then jumped to her shoulder.

It was all there, yet it wasn't. Something was wrong, false, about the scene.

The woman turned from the table and started toward me. She looked into my eyes and reached out her hand.

"You're Bombast's sister," I screamed. "You're dressed up. It's a trick!"

"Joshua!" a voice cried on the steps behind me.

I whirled around.

It was Angela. A woman was holding her arm behind her in a hammerlock. She was the woman with the weird sunglasses and the scarf. She was the woman we thought was Bombast's sister. She was the woman we thought had dressed up as the ghost.

Then who was the woman in the hall?

"RUN, JOSHUA!" Angela screamed.

At that, Shackleford broke away and ran into the hall. I blew my whistle as loud as I could, then turned and ran after her ... straight down the long hallway ... straight toward the beckoning ghost.

13

It was the strangest moment of my life: hurtling down a hallway *toward* a ghost.

Obviously, I hadn't thought it out.

I mean I didn't say to myself — hmm, ghost up ahead, weird sunglasses-wearing woman behind, sister warning me to run, dog running — hmmm, I believe I'll run.

Obviously, I didn't have time for that. If I had, maybe I'd have tried running UP the stairs instead of DOWN the hall after Shackleford. Maybe; who knows?

The princess just stared at me, as if frozen by surprise. She didn't move at all, but she seemed to grow, looming larger and larger as I ran.

Jack the monkey stared and grew, too.

When I'd first caught sight of him two seconds before he'd looked normal monkey-size, just as he'd looked in the castle window the night before. Now he looked as big as a chimpanzee and was bucking for gorilla.

And the wild chattering — it was everywhere. Noise whirled around me and swamped my brain. Angela screaming, Shackleford barking, Jack chattering, my heart pounding.

Suddenly, Jack jumped right into my arms, nearly giving me a heart attack. He was monkey-size again, and he threw both arms around my neck, buried his head in my shoulder and held on.

And yet ... the giant Jack the monkey was still twenty feet away at the end of the hall, still staring.

Just then, Shackleford reached the princess, ran smack into her and bounced off. That's right, bounced off.

I skidded to a halt beside the door to THE room, the one with the window fourth from the end. It was ajar. In desperation, I darted into the dark room with Jack still clinging to my neck. Shackleford dashed in behind me.

I pushed the door shut and tried to lock it, but someone was pushing hard on the other side.

I leaned against the door with all the strength I could muster while being strangled by a monkey.

It was no use.

Slowly, the door pushed open with me, Jack and Shackleford attached. A figure plunged inside the pitch black room.

Then the door slammed shut and someone turned a key on the other side.

* * * *

Jack let go of me and bounded over to the dark figure picking herself up off the floor.

"There, there, Jack, it's OK," a soft voice said.

It was Angela.

"Whoa," I said, collapsing on the floor in relief. "I'm glad it's you. I thought I was locked in here with Princess Elizabeth."

"Don't relax yet," Angela said. "We've got to get out of here fast. She may come back for us.

"Have you still got your flashlight and whistle?" she asked. "Weird Sunglasses took mine."

I flipped on my flashlight. Shackleford had stopped shaking and was sniffing around Jack, which didn't sit well with Jack at all. He scampered around Angela's shoulders and hopped on her head where he scolded Shackleford and shook his long, bony finger.

Shackleford looked dumbfounded.

"He's awfully lively for a ghost monkey," I said.

Angela laughed. "He's no ghost. Jack is a genuine live monkey. That I'm sure of."

"Does he bite?" I asked.

"He hasn't yet," Angela said. "I'll keep Jack and Shackleford apart. You go over to the window and blow your whistle."

The window was locked tight. I pressed against it and peered into the night, but the floodlights shining on the castle were blinding.

I hammered on the window and blew my whistle. Six hammers, three blows, six hammers, three blows, six hammers, three blows.

"You're breaking my eardrums, Joshua," Angela said

finally. "Let's take a two-minute break and compare notes."

The furniture had been covered with blankets again, so I sat down on a dusty floor and leaned against the door.

I glanced at my watch. It was 9:40 p.m. Soon "The Student Prince" would be over, and all the tourists would leave for the night. I hoped Supergranny could spring us before that. The castle was spooky enough as it was.

"What's going on in that hall?" I asked Angela.

"Beats me," she said. "I was climbing the stairs in the dark with you right behind me — at least, I *thought* you were right behind me ..."

She frowned. "Where were you, anyway? We were supposed to stick together."

"Schackleford problems," I said, glaring at Schackleford, who was now being as nice as pie, trying to make friends with Jack.

I almost pointed out to Angela that it takes two to stick together, and if she hadn't forged up the steps without us, this might not have happened. But I didn't. We were in enough trouble without wasting time arguing.

"Go on, what happened?" I prodded.

"Well, I thought you were right behind me. When I turned around to ask you which floor we wanted, it wasn't you. It was Weird Sunglasses carrying Jack in his basket cage.

"She grabbed me, ripped my whistle string over my head, and held me in a hammerlock with one hand over my mouth. But in the process she dropped Jack's basket and he bolted.

"She held me in the hallway one floor down while you and Schackleford went up past us."

"Do you think *IT* is still out there?" I asked. I meant the princess, of course.

"I don't know," Angela said. "*IT* was when Weird Sunglasses pushed me in here. Can you see anything through the crack under the door?"

I pressed my face to the crack. The door fit tight, but surely a little light would have shone through if *IT* were still out there.

"I think *IT* is gone," I whispered. "There's no light under the door. I hope *IT* doesn't show up in here."

I'd seen enough of Princess Elizabeth for one night. All I needed was for her to spring up in a corner, glowing in candlelight and larger than life.

"*IT* won't," Angela said. "And even if *IT* does, *IT* is not a ghost. *IT* is some kind of trick."

"Ghost or trick, I hope *IT* doesn't come in here," I said, trying not to think of the strange, staring woman looming ahead of me on my sprint down the hall.

"Go give the whistle another try," Angela said.

By now Jack had climbed down from Angela's head. He was holding on to Angela's neck with one bony paw and leaning down to scratch Shackleford behind the ear with the other.

I was glad they were making friends. Being locked up in a haunted castle was bad enough without having to break up a dog and monkey fight.

I went to the window and hit the whistle again.

But just then somebody pounded on the heavy door.

"Joshua, Angela, Shackleford? Are you in there?"

It was Supergranny to the rescue!

14

"Let's go over this wall one more time," Supergranny said.

We were standing in the empty hall. Empty, that is, except for Supergranny, Herr Hinkel, Angela, Vannie, Shackleford, Chesterton, Jack and me.

The candlelight, table, tapestries, Princess Elizabeth and giant monkey had disappeared. So had Weird Sunglasses. It was just a common, ordinary, sixty-foot-long stone castle hall.

Supergranny had dragged Herr Hinkel upstairs to spring us as soon as she heard my whistle.

Now Herr Hinkel, Angela, Vannie and I were all shining flashlights on the wall at the end of the hall where we'd seen the princess. Supergranny was tapping every inch of it she could reach with her knuckles. The parts she couldn't reach she tapped with the folding pointer she always carried in her purse.

"Aha!" she said. "It's a stone wall, all right. No secret doorway. No secret window. No hollow spots. No wonder Shackleford bounced off. It's solid stone clear through. Good."

We didn't know what was good about it, but we didn't interrupt her train of thought to ask. Time was running out.

While Angela and I had been locked in the castle, something very strange had happened:

The ghost had reappeared to the tourists on the terrace.

"Supergranny and I were milling around on the terrace, still looking for Bombast," Vannie said. "Just as we spotted him a few feet away, there she was again. It was a rerun of last night. Same scream, same monkey, same window, everything."

"Three New York publishers saw it," Supergranny added. "They flew in today to talk about buying the diary and were on the terrace when she appeared.

"They each offered Bombast a million dollars on the spot for the princess's diary. He announced he would decide tonight which offer to accept. He'll meet the publishers at the Oberunterhof at 10 a.m. tomorrow to sign the contract.

"It's 10 p.m. now, so we have only twelve hours to stop one of the biggest scams in history," Supergranny said.

"Yes," Vannie said, looking at her watch. "It's been twenty minutes exactly since the ghost appeared. I remember checking the time. It was 9:40 p.m."

My hands, feet and blood turned cold.

"But it couldn't have happened then," I rasped. "*I* was

standing at the window at 9:40 p.m. The second I sat down I looked at my watch."

Are you both sure about the time?" Supergranny asked quickly.

Vannie and I nodded.

"Wonderful," she said, hugging us. "You were so smart to check the time. It's all falling into place."

I didn't know what was so smart about it; nothing was falling into place for me. But there was no time to dwell on it because Supergranny began debriefing Angela and me.

She made us go through everything we'd seen since starting Plan 432B. Three times. Weird Sunglasses, glowing candlelight, the princess getting bigger, Jack jumping into my arms, Shackleford bouncing off the princess, blinding floodlights ... the whole spiel.

"Aha," she'd say every now and then. "Good!"

Finally she finished debriefing us and inspecting the wall. She folded the pointer and stuck it back in her purse.

"Well, we know the light couldn't have come from behind the wall, because it's solid. Let's check upstairs."

Herr Hinkel locked *THE* room, and we all trooped to the other end of the hall and up the stairs.

"Everybody get down on hands and knees and look for it," Supergranny said. "Use your flashlights. It should be about the size of a placemat."

Everybody except Shackleford, Chesterton and Jack, who were starting a game of "Herd the Monkey," got down on their knees. Even Herr Hinkel. I wondered if he understood what was going on; I didn't have a clue what she was looking for, and I speak English.

"Er, Supergranny," Vannie said, "what are we looking for?"

Supergranny looked up blankly. "Oh, sorry. I thought you'd figured it out. The hole, of course. Probably a rectangle. About as big as a placemat."

Thirty seconds later Angela found it. A piece of stone about the size of a placemat had been cut out of the floor, then fit back into place.

It fit so snugly you could barely see the crack, even with five flashlights shining on it.

Supergranny wedged the extra-strength screwdriver she carries everywhere into the crack and pried the stone up a couple of inches.

"Grab it," she gasped.

Guard Hinkel and I got our hands under the stone and hefted it up. We pointed our flashlights into the hole and could see clear through to the hallway below.

Two steel brackets across the bottom of the hole had kept the stone from falling clear through to the hallway below.

"Clever," Supergranny said. "Devilishly clever. I hadn't thought of the steel brackets. But, of course, they needed a way to support the stone after they'd cut it out. I suppose they hung the projector from the brackets, too."

"Projector?" Angela asked.

"The slide projector," Supergranny answered. "They must have hung the projector on a small platform. Attached it to those steel brackets, I'd guess."

"What slide projector?" I asked.

"The one for 'The Ghost of Heidelberg Castle' slide show, of course," she said, staring at us in amazement.

"You mean you hadn't figured that out, either?"

Nobody said anything. Herr Hinkel coughed.

She laughed. "Never mind, I'll explain it all on the way back to Oberunterdorf. We've got an all-nighter ahead of us.

"*We* know the ghost of Heidelberg Castle is one giant slide-show fraud. The question is: Can we prove it by 10 o'clock tomorrow?"

15

"Let's sit on the stairs and flesh out Plan 72X," Super-granny said. "I don't want to get up to Oberunterdorf and find we need something from Heidelberg. You can't always find everything you need in a tiny village like Oberunter-dorf at 11 o'clock at night. And we've got too much to do to be running up and down the Odenwald all night."

We all sat down with Shackleford, Chesterton and Jack on the bottom step, as chummy as three musketeers.

"I could kick myself for not bringing my slide projector from the States," Supergranny said. "Plan 72X absolutely requires a slide projector, and I didn't pack mine. It was right in my suitcase with its adapter to make it work on German electricity, and I took it out.

"It comes from reading too many of those newspaper travel advice columns. They're forever telling you to pack half as much as you think you'll need. I know darned good and well you always need five times what you think you'll need. Here we are, desperate for a slide projector, and I didn't pack mine. I hope this will be a lesson to me."

"*Auf Deutsch, bitte?*"[1] Herr Hinkel said. He was asking her to repeat it in German, which she did. At least, I guess she did. She rattled on for some time in German. Then Herr Hinkel started rattling back, and both of them got excited and started yelling, "*Ja, ja*"[2] and "*Gut, gut.*"[3]

"Well, we're saved this time," she said to us. "He'll loan us his slide projector if we stop by his apartment on the way back to Oberunterdorf. I wonder if he happens to have a long, green dress and red wig to fit Angela?"

He didn't, but she said she thought she could get that from Meg.

We went over a few more details, then filed down the stairs. Herr Hinkel carefully locked the castle door, and we walked silently across the deserted courtyard.

*　　　*　　　*　　　*

As soon as we picked up Herr Hinkel's slide projector, we headed for the hills.

The old owl was still waiting for us in the tall pine in the meadow.

This time I was kind of glad to see him. He flapped across

---

1. *Auf Deutsch, bitte.* Sounds like "Owf Doych, bitta." Means "In German, please?"
2. *Ja.* Sounds like "Ya." Means "yes."
3. *Gut.* Sounds like "goot." Means "good."

the road, then hooted from behind as we wound our way to the village.

"I think he's playing 'Herd the Porsche,' " Vannie said.

We went straight to Oma's room when we got to the Oberunterhof.

She opened the door wearing her long, blue robe and the fuzzy rabbit slippers we'd brought her from the States. She had taken her gray hair out of the bun, and it hung halfway down her back.

She seemed kind of surprised to see us, especially Jack, but she insisted we come in for hot chocolate while Supergranny updated her on Bombast and Ghost.

The more she heard, the madder she got.

When Supergranny reached the part about Bombast signing the contract at the Oberunterhof the next morning, she clanged her chocolate cup down in the saucer in disgust.

"The nerve of that slimy Bombast," she said. "After what he did to his dear old cousin! Now he's trying to use *our* Oberunterhof in one of his scams! And telling a million-dollar lie about our beautiful Heidelberg Castle and the poor, dear princess, bless her soul."

But would she help us with Plan 72X?

"You bet!" she said. "*Doch!*[1] *Gern!*[2] You bet!"

"Great," Supergranny said. "We'll use your room as Command Post." She looked at her watch. "Good heavens, it's almost midnight; we've got to get rolling.

"First, we must locate Bombast, then one of us has to get into his room."

---

1. *Doch.* Rhymes with "soak." Means "yes, indeed."
2. *Gern.* Rhymes with "chair'n." Means "gladly."

I groaned. Something told me I'd be elected to sneak into Bombast's room.

"It's going to be me, isn't it?" I asked. "I'm going to be the one who has to sneak into Bombast's room."

"Probably," Supergranny said. "First, we have to find out if he has turned in for the night."

"He was still drinking schnapps and playing skat in the dining room when I came upstairs," Oma said. "It's *freiwilliger*[1] fire department meeting night. After their meeting they always stop in to play cards. When Bombast got back from Heidelberg tonight he joined the game."

"Good," Supergranny said. "If he's still there our job will be easier."

She dispatched Angela and Vannie to the dining room to check.

"Now, props," Supergranny said as soon as they left. "We need a monkey and a long, green dress and red wig to fit Angela. We've already got the monkey. Oma, can you come up with the dress and wig?"

Oma thought a dress and wig Meg had worn to a costume party might work. "It's in the attic. Toss me one of those flashlights, and I'll go after it."

Supergranny tossed her a flashlight. On her way out, Oma handed me a chocolate coin wrapped in gold paper and a pass key.

Every night she turned down each Oberunterhof guest's bed and put a piece of chocolate candy on the pillow. She'd already done it for that night, of course.

---

1.   *Freiwilliger.* Sounds like "Fry villy grr." Means "volunteer." In this case, volunteer firefighter.

"But maybe I forgot Bombast's room; I can't remember, Joshua. Maybe you should do it for me." She winked and was out the door.

By then Vannie was back to report that Bombast was still downing schnapps and playing cards. "He's dealing. Angela is at the door. If he starts to get up, she'll signal by snapping her fingers three times."

"Excellent," Supergranny said. "Vannie, park yourself halfway up the steps. If Angela signals, cough three times. If I hear you cough, I'll have Shackleford signal.

"Joshua, if you hear Shackleford's signal, hightail it out of Bombast's room. Got it?"

"Got it," I groaned.

She gave me a quick rundown on what to look for in Bombast's room, then shoved me out the door.

Most of the guests were already asleep, and the hallway was very still. Nobody was in sight unless you count the shadow of Vannie crouched on the stairs.

I tiptoed up the next flight and crossed the hall to Bombast's room, trying to remember two things:

1. Be quiet and move fast so nobody would see me.

2. Be casual like a guest-house employee delivering chocolates and turning down beds.

It was hard to do both at once, but I tried.

Still trying to be quiet, quick and casual, I pressed my ear against Bombast's door. If anyone was inside, he was zombie quiet. I fit the pass key in the lock. Mercifully, it turned.

I pushed the door lever down and slipped into Bombast's dark and empty room.

16

The room was tidy. You could say that much for Bombast. He might be a liar, thief and cheat, but he was a *neat* liar, thief and cheat.

My flashlight beam played across the room, touching the chocolate Oma had placed on Bombast's pillow earlier, his spit-shined extra pair of shoes lined up beside his slippers, and the heavy, wooden wardrobe on the wall opposite the bed.

A German book was on the nightstand.

It had a picture of Princess Elizabeth in her later years on the cover. No doubt he was reading up on her — the better to fool the entire world.

The princess wore dangling earrings, a high lace collar, and a dark, heavy-looking dress. She was holding an ostrich feather fan, and she didn't look nearly as pretty as she had in the castle. She had thin lips, a long, important-looking nose and eyes that were looking straight at me. Unlike the rest of the picture, the eyes seemed alive.

Enough!

I didn't want to dwell on *her* anymore. I took another quick look around the room. The wardrobe seemed the best bet for the camera case and slides, and that was what I was after: one special slide.

"Try to find the one of Elizabeth and Jack in the castle window," Supergranny had said. "That's the one we really need. If you can't find it, get whatever you think is next best. Use your own judgment."

I hate it when she says that — "Use your own judgment." What judgment? I wasn't even supposed to be up this late, much less sneaking around a German count's bedroom searching for a picture of a ghost. How did I know what was "next best"?

I tiptoed across the room and opened one of the wardrobe doors.

It creaked loud enough to wake up all Oberunterdorf. I froze and waited for someone in the next room to pound on the wall and start yelling whatever the German is for "Quiet in there."

But nothing happened.

This section of the wardrobe was a bust. Bombast's raincoat, spare suit, pajamas and robe hung straight as soldiers at attention. His olive green felt hat sat smack in the middle on the shelf above. The floor under the wardrobe was empty.

I couldn't face closing the incredibly creaky door just yet, so I left it open and moved on to the next one.

This time I struck gold: a camera bag and boxes of slide trays stacked on shelves. Actually, it was more gold than I'd hoped for or wanted. There were three boxes of slide trays.

Drat.

One box would have been plenty. I hadn't counted on sifting through three. There were enough pictures for a twelve-hour miniseries.

I pulled out the first box and got to work, holding each slide up in front of my flashlight, then putting it back in its tray wrongside-out and backward just as it had come out.

There were slides of the princess in the garden beside the Neptune fountain, under the Elizabeth gate, on the terrace and inside the castle.

There were slides of the princess with and without Jack. Slides of furniture in elegant rooms. Slides of elegant rooms without furniture. Slides and more slides. More and more and more slides.

I limped through Tray One and started Tray Two.

If you've ever tried looking at 400 slides with a flashlight at 1 a.m., you know what it does. It makes you sleepy. Sleepier than you have ever been. Sleepier than you ever thought possible. It could wipe out the entire sleeping pill industry in three nights.

My eyes started closing and my head kept jerking forward.

"I've got to lie down," I thought. "Just for a minute."

I stretched out on my side and stuck the flashlight in one of Bombast's shoes with the light propped up over the heel. Then I held each slide in front of the light with one hand.

The slides were starting to act up. They wouldn't go back in the tray right. They kept missing the slot. Then the same one would keep coming up again and again. Then I'd lose my place and have to start over.

"Wake up," I kept telling myself. "You can't go to sleep right in the middle of Bombast's floor."

At last I got through Tray Two.

I started on Tray Three.

One, two, three, four, thirty-five, forty-seven slides from Tray Three. Still no slide of the princess and Jack in the window. I was starting to panic — sort of a sleepy panic.

I stuck a slide in my pocket. I didn't know if it would turn out to be "next best" to the slide of the princess in the window, but after all this I had to leave with something. Ten slides later another "next best" contender popped up. What the heck, I stuck it in my pocket, too.

Only ten more slides to go. Maybe I'd make it. Surely I could stay awake for ten more slides.

Bingo! Eighth-to-the-last was it. I stuck it in my pocket, put Bombast's shoe back under the bed, and started to slip Tray Three under the other two boxes on the shelf.

But what was that? That noise?

I paused with my hand still on the box of slides.

I thought I'd heard a dog bark. Everything was silent, then there were three sharp barks from Shackleford.

It was the signal.

Most people would think Shackleford was just doing some all-purpose barking, but it was really Command Post telling me Bombast was on his way.

We had spent an entire weekend in Supergranny's kitchen teaching Shackleford the signal in case we ever needed it. As it turned out, we needed it about twice a week.

I had to get out of there fast.

I turned to make a quick exit, but my hand caught Slide Tray Three and pulled it off the shelf.

It bounced open and one-hundred and forty slides leaped out.

Voices were coming from downstairs — probably Bombast and the *freiwilligers*[1] saying goodnight.

If he found this mess, our game was up; no way would we be able to spring our trap.

Cursing slides, wardrobes and myself, I knelt and began cramming slides back into the tray.

---

1. *Freiwilliger.* Sounds like "Fry villy grr." Means "volunteer." In this case, volunteer firefighter.

17

A door slammed downstairs, and the sounds of the *freiwilligers'*[1] laughter moved outside, then died away as they drifted home.

Footsteps were coming up the stairs.

I reached for the last scattered puddle of slides by the window and stuffed them into the tray.

Footsteps were on the landing.

I carefully slipped the tray back on the shelf and bolted for the door.

Too late!

Bombast was fumbling with the lock.

I dashed back to the wardrobe, stepped inside the section with Bombast's suits and raincoat, and pulled the

---

1. *Freiwilliger.* Sounds like "Fry villy grr." Means "volunteer." In this case, volunteer firefighter.

creaking door shut just as he opened the door and switched on the light.

I shrank back into the corner of the wardrobe behind the clothes.

What now?

At least I was awake. The *pain* took care of that. I'd landed all wrong and was afraid to move. All my weight was on one foot, my neck pressed against the corner at an odd angle, and everything hurt. But one move would set the empty coat hangers singing, "Joshua's in the wardrobe, Joshua's in the wardrobe."

I heard the bed creak as Bombast sat down.

Thud, one shoe hit the floor.

Thud, there went another.

Silence. Superneat Bombast was probably lining up his shoes with a ruler.

I heard him stand up, then scuff across the floor in his slippers.

He was heading for the bathroom!

He closed the bathroom door and turned the lock!

He had locked himself in the bathroom!

He turned on the faucet!

I was saved! Maybe.

I had to make my move. Slowly, I opened the incredible creaking wardrobe door, praying that he wouldn't hear it above the running water.

I waited three seconds, dashed for the loor, locked it from the outside, then slid down the bannister to Oma's room.

*   *   *   *

Boy, were they glad to see me at Command Post.

"As soon as we realized you were trapped in Bombast's room, we started a rescue mission," Vannie said. "But we didn't think it would work."

"Great," I said sarcastically. "That makes me feel much better."

Oma had already gone downstairs to start the rescue mission, which was to be a fire drill. She was using the phone at Meg's desk in the dining room to call the *freiwilliger*[1] fire department captain and ask him to come back to the Oberunterhof to run the fire drill.

Angela raced downstairs to stop her.

"The idea was that all the guests, including Bombast, would have to leave the building when the alarm went off," Supergranny said. "We hoped that you'd catch on that it was a rescue attempt, stay put until Bombast left, then run for it."

She said all that with her teeth shut, because she had a bunch of straight pins in her mouth. She had been sitting in the middle of the floor, pinning up the long, green dress Angela was wearing.

As soon as Oma and Angela returned, Angela went back to her place in the middle of the room and turned slowly while Supergranny finished pinning up the dress.

It was the old costume Meg had worn to a party, and Angela was supposed to look like Princess Elizabeth in it. But she still looked like Angela to me.

"Er, I hate to be negative," I said, "but do you really think this will fool Bombast?"

---

1. *Freiwilliger.* Sounds like "Fry villy grr." Means "volunteer." In this case, volunteer firefighter.

Supergranny tilted her head to the left and looked at Angela.

Then she tilted her head to the right and looked at Angela.

"Oh, well, not yet, Joshua," she said. "But we're not finished by miles. By the time we add a little makeup, a wig, a sheer screen, and dark room, Prince Frederick himself would be fooled."

She cocked her head to the left again. "I hope."

Then she snapped her head to attention and clapped her hands. "Now, action!"

"Angela, change back into your jeans and practice your lines."

"Roger," Angela said.

"Oma, please hem up the dress where I've pinned it."

"OK," Oma said.

"Vannie, keep rehearsing with Jack. Have you got plenty of dried banana bits?"

"Yep," Vannie said, patting her pocket. "Half a pocket full." (We were teaching Jack his part in the show by giving him a banana bit every time he did something right.)

"Shackleford and Chesterton, stay out of trouble," Supergranny said.

They were both snoozing beside Oma's rocking chair and didn't hear her.

"Joshua, come with me. We'll set up."

She looked at her watch. "It's 1:30 a.m., and show time is 2:30 a.m. As soon as Joshua and I get back, I'll do Angela's makeup, and we'll have one quick rehearsal. Got it?"

Everybody nodded, and we were off.

Our first stop was the Oberunterhof kitchen.

"We're going to have to improvise," Supergranny whispered. "If we were home, we'd just pop into my workshop-office-laboratory-playroom-garage and get all the equipment we need for Plan 72X."

You may already know about Supergranny's workshop-office-laboratory-playroom-garage. If so, you probably already know that I think it's the best room in the world. I think you could look for 137 years and never find a better one.

It was quite a shock for me, the first time I saw it.

We'd just moved in from Cleveland and I had come over hunting for Shackleford, who had blundered out of our yard by mistake.

There I was dog hunting, and accidentally discovered Supergranny's secret room behind the fireplace. You just eat a snickerdoodle cookie with the magic ingredient, push a yellow button by the fireplace, and, whammo, the fireplace opens and "Stars and Stripes Forever" booms out of the ceiling.

It's where she keeps the Ferrari, Chesterton, the helicopter pad, swimming pool, vending machines, world maps and almost everything else.

And equipment?

Tons of equipment.

"Yes, if we were home, we'd just pop into my office and pick up everything we need for Plan 72X," Supergranny repeated.

"But since we're 6,000 miles from home, we'll have to improvise."

She rubbed her hands together and grinned.

"Sometimes I just *love* to improvise, don't you? It's such nice exercise for the brain."

I nodded.

"Good," she said. "Then start looking for a wooden cutting board about the size of a placemat while I get a large kettle."

The first cutting board I found was too small, but I found another one just the right size tucked in a narrow cabinet beside the sink.

Meanwhile, Supergranny lifted a shiny, tin-looking kettle down from a rack above the stove.

"Perfect," she murmured. "Now, to the toolshed."

We picked up a ladder and long, outdoor extension cord from the toolshed.

Carrying ladder, extension cord, kettle, cutting board, Supergranny's purse, and Herr Hinkel's slide projector, we approached the oak tree outside Bombast's window.

We carefully leaned the ladder against the tree, and Supergranny put scissors and a roll of extra-strength grosgrain ribbon she carries everywhere in the kettle.

I slipped the kettle's handle over my shoulder and started up the ladder.

My job was to climb out onto the limb nearest Bombast's window.

"I'd do it, but I'm too big," Supergranny whispered. "I might break the limb."

Sure, I thought to myself, rolling my eyes. I knew she couldn't see me rolling my eyes in the dark.

The limb was fairly thick, about as big around as a telephone pole at the spot near Bombast's window, which was as far out as I had to go.

I straddled the limb, tied a long piece of grosgrain ribbon to the kettle handle, then slowly let the kettle down to the ground. She put the cutting board in it, and I reeled it up.

I tied the cutting board to the limb with the grosgrain ribbon, then let the kettle down again and reeled up Herr Hinkel's projector, which suddenly seemed to weigh five hundred pounds.

I tied the projector down to the cutting board, which was to be our projector table. I was careful not to let the ribbon get in front of the lens. Then I let the kettle down again.

Next, I plugged in the projector's remote control, and inched back to the tree trunk, carrying the remote switch in my hand.

I tied it to a branch and signaled Supergranny that we were ready for the test.

She unreeled the extension cord and plugged it into the outdoor outlet near the balcony that Rolf always used for Christmas lights.

I flipped the remote switch and the projector's motor hummed.

I pushed "forward" and the slide tray clicked forward.

I signaled "thumbs up" to Supergranny.

The test had worked.

"So far, so good," Supergranny whispered as I climbed down the ladder. "Now, I'll do Angela's makeup while you and Vannie get into your black outfits and put black stage paint on your faces.

"Rehearsal in ten minutes!"

18

At 2:30 a.m. on the nose we locked Shackleford and Chesterton in Oma's room and lined up in the hall.

"Check your watches," Supergranny whispered.

We checked our watches. Everybody had 2:30 a.m. on the nose.

Supergranny shook our hands and Jack's paw.

"Good luck," she said. "Remember, the curtain goes up at two hoots."

She meant the signal to start was two owl hoots. Not real owl hoots, of course; Supergranny-in-tree-pretending-to-be-an-owl hoots.

"Places, everyone," she said, disappearing down the stairs.

The rest of us — Angela dressed as Princess Elizabeth with Jack on her shoulder, Vannie and I dressed in all black like mimes in a shadow theater, and Oma dressed as herself — trooped up the stairs to Bombast's room. Vannie and I were carrying a screen Oma had made from a sheer lace curtain.

The hall was very dark.

We all leaned against Bombast's door to listen. He was snoring a funny, shaky snore with chirps at the end. It started low, then shakily climbed in pitch and ended with three little chirps.

Oma quietly fit the key in the lock and pushed the door lever. She patted each of us on the head for luck and put her finger to her lips to remind Jack to be quiet.

Jack put his own bony finger to his lips. He was either a prize mimic or a very smart monkey; I hadn't quite decided which.

The four of us, counting Jack, slipped into the room. Oma closed the door behind us and waited in the hall.

There I was again.

I'd sure seen enough of that room to last a lifetime.

Bombast snored on. He was really out of it. Maybe it was all the schnapps he'd drunk, but whatever it was, he was out of it. "Snoooooooor chrrp, chrrrp, chrrrppp," he went. "Snooooooorp, chrrp, chrrrp, chrrrppp."

We took our places in front of the wardrobe, and Vannie and I held the curtain screen. We wore black makeup on our faces and black gloves in addition to black jeans and sweatshirts. The idea was for us to blend into the dark room so Bombast wouldn't see us. Angela stood behind the screen.

We were just in time.

Two hoots came from the tree outside the window. That

meant Supergranny had made it up the tree and was sitting in the branches holding the projector's remote control switch.

Hardly had the hooting died away when the projector light flipped on, shining straight through the window onto our screen. There were no slides showing yet — that came in Part 2.

Angela playing the princess was Part 1 of this little drama, and we just needed the projector light as a spotlight for now.

Bombast flounced over on his stomach when the light came on and pulled the pillow over his head.

"Snooooooooor chrrppp, chrrppp, chrrppp," he went again.

"Bommmmmbaasst," a soft voice called. It was so spooky, I jumped. I *knew* it was Angela, but I couldn't help it, I still jumped.

"Bommmmmbaasst," she called again.

I wished I could see how she looked behind the screen.

In fact, I couldn't stand it. I *had* to see how she looked behind the screen.

I bobbed my head in front just a second.

She looked like a genuine ghost, that's how she looked. You could see the green of her dress and the red of her hair. And yet the curtain made it all look strange, not quite there, floating.

I pulled my head back behind the screen where it belonged.

"BOMMMMMBAASSSTTT," she crooned, louder.

That did it.

"Whhhha--?" Bombast grunted, raising his head about

six inches from the pillow. "WHHHHHA--?" he yelled, sitting straight up in bed.

"Bommmmmbaasssttt," Angela crooned again.

This was it. This was the minute he could burst out laughing, jump up, turn on the light, grab the screen, and cart us off to jail.

He didn't.

His mouth flew open. His eyes bulged. He clutched the feather cover to his chin.

I stopped worrying he'd catch on and started worrying he'd have a heart attack.

He didn't.

"You liiiieeed," Angela said, her voice soft and eerie and full of venom. "You liiiieeed."

"No, no," Bombast blubbered. "No, Your Highness, no, no."

"The diary," she hissed. "Give me the diary!"

Bombast just stared, frozen in place.

"THE DIARY," Angela hissed.

"Yes, yes, Your Majesty," Bombast blubbered. He reached under his pillow and pulled out a book. He held it outstretched.

"Here, anything, just please go away," he pleaded. "Please leave me alone."

Angela raised her hand slowly, ghostlike, and touched Jack's ear. It was the signal for Supergranny, watching through the window, to turn off the light and for Jack to dive for the diary.

Instantly, the projector light switched off and Jack jumped down from Angela's shoulder and scampered across the room. He hopped onto Bombast's bed, lay a letter on the nightstand, and grabbed the diary, sending Bombast into a screaming spasm.

"Get away from me, go away, go away!" he screeched, diving under the covers and pulling the pillow over his head.

It was not a pretty sight, and the uproar stirred up the guests next door, who started pounding on the wall.

Good ol' Jack whirled back behind the screen and jumped into Angela's arms carrying what we hoped would be the fake diary that would *not* rewrite 17th-century history.

It was time to exit.

Before Bombast came to his senses.

Before the people next door came barreling in.

Before Bombast noticed a gray-haired bespectacled woman in the tree outside his window.

We slipped toward the door as quietly as we could under cover of darkness and Bombast's babbling.

Just as we pulled the door shut, the projector light went on again with Part 2 of our little drama.

This time the slide of the fake princess and Jack flashed onto the wardrobe. The idea was to cover our exit and give Bombast something to think about when he woke up all the way, sobered up, stopped shaking, and realized he hadn't really seen a ghost.

What we wanted him to think about was this:

Somebody was onto his little caper and had a slide to prove it. They also had the fake diary.

That's what we wanted him to think about ... and that's when we hoped he'd sign the paper on his nightstand.

19

It was 5 minutes till 3 by the time I got back to my room, washed the black stuff off my face, changed into pajamas and climbed into bed.

"Oboy," I thought, "six whole hours to sleep."

We were due at breakfast at 9 a.m. "Nine sharp," Supergranny had said. I figured if I got up at 5 minutes till 9, I could make it. I closed my eyes to start my six hours sleep.

Ha!

Who could sleep after what we'd been through? Who could sleep with Vannie and Angela still thumping around in the next room?

I wished they would settle down. Plan 72X called for us to jump into bed and pretend we'd been asleep for hours in case Bombast got up and started snooping through the halls.

Why tip him off that we were still up? Attract attention? All that?

Finally they settled down.

It didn't help.

Too many pictures raced through my mind: Weird Sunglasses grabbing for me, Angela screaming, Shackleford and me running down the castle hall, Princess Elizabeth looming bigger and bigger, Jack sitting on Angela's head, Supergranny tapping the wall with her pointer, the owl playing "Herd the Porsche," 40 million slides falling on my head, Supergranny in a tree, Bombast bolting up in bed ... on and on they went, round and round, unstoppable.

My eyes wouldn't stay shut.

What was Bombast doing now? Had he sobered up and figured out *we* had haunted his room? Was he outside my door this minute? Would he burst in to search for the diary?

Or did he have another copy of the fake diary? Had he been playing us along? Was he having a good laugh somewhere right now with his spooky sister?

Would he go ahead and sign the million-dollar deal at 10 a.m. after all? Or had we stopped the scam of the century?

We'd taken a couple of minutes to look over the diary in Oma's room. It *looked* old, all right. Oma thought it might be based on research work of the old professor — the one Bombast had swindled years ago. At any rate, the paper was brown and crumbly and the writing was old-fashioned English mixed with old-fashioned German. It was very hard to read.

Supergranny had hidden it, and she wouldn't tell us where.

"Go to bed and don't worry your heads about it," she said. "The less you know about that the better."

Finally, I fell asleep.

It was worse than being awake. A man with a red mustache was chasing me, but I couldn't run fast. It was like I was running through Jell-O. The giant face of a woman in weird sunglasses loomed out of the sky. The man kept gaining on me. I could feel his bony fingers grabbing my shirt. Suddenly, Princess Elizabeth blocked my path. She reached out her hand. She was screaming.

I awoke, my heart pounding. The room was filled with sunlight. I looked at the clock; it was 5 minutes till 9.

*   *   *   *

Vannie, Angela and I slid into our chairs at the breakfast table at the same time. Oma and Supergranny, who was holding Baby Sadie wrapped in a light blanket, were already there drinking coffee.

Our table was on the balcony overlooking the parking lot *and* Bombast's maroon Mercedes.

"Rats, he's still here," Vannie muttered.

"Don't panic yet," Supergranny said. "We've got an hour. If he leaves before time to sign the deal at 10 a.m., we're still on target."

Meg brought us juice, milk and rolls while Supergranny rehashed the crime.

"You gave me the key, Oma," she said, "when you mentioned Bombast put black paper over his bathroom window.

"I asked myself, *why*?"

"To make a darkroom to develop pictures?" Angela asked.

"Exactly," Supergranny answered. "Then when we got Carl's call about Bombast's beautiful sister getting out of jail, three things fell into place:

"1. We'd seen the woman in weird sunglasses taking an unholy number of pictures at the castle.

2. We'd seen her lunching with Bombast at the Ritter.

3. We'd seen a long, bony finger wave to us from a basket under her chair."

"Jack's finger," Vannie put in. "A monkey just like the real Princess Elizabeth's 350 years ago."

"Precisely," Supergranny said. "I suspected that underneath the weird sunglasses and scarf was Bombast's beautiful sister."

"A ringer for the princess," I said.

"Right," Supergranny said. "She probably dressed like the princess, then sashayed around the castle gardens at dusk to stir up interest."

"She sure stirred up Shackleford and Chesterton's interest," I said.

Everybody laughed.

"She probably hid in the storage room to get away from Shackleford and Chesterton," Supergranny went on. "Then when we went for Herr Hinkel, she slipped out."

"But how did Bombast make the ghost?" Vannie asked.

"It was all pictures — slides projected onto the castle," Supergranny said.

"I think he had two projectors in the cases he took to the castle last night," she said slowly. "The first probably went on a platform in the trees beneath the castle with its lens aimed at *THE* room. I'd guess it ran on a generator and was set by a timer to turn on at 9:40 p.m."

"Bombast probably set up the platform in advance," Angela said. "Then, all he had to do last night was quickly put the projector in place and dash back to the castle terrace," Angela said.

"Undoubtedly," Supergranny agreed. "He could easily have been back on the terrace when the slide flashed on, making it appear that the princess and Jack were at the window."

Dawn broke. "So what I thought were floodlights shining in my eyes at the window was actually the projector light?" I asked.

"Of course," Supergranny said. "Bombast probably fixed the floodlights to turn off when his projector turned on. Timing was crucial to his scheme."

"What about the second projector?" Angela asked.

"We found the spot in the hallway where it was to be used, of course," Supergranny said. "I think you, Joshua and Shackleford surprised Weird Sunglasses in the middle of a practice show. They probably planned to lure the publishers up there later to really convince them that the castle was haunted and seal the deal."

"And pry even more money out of them," Oma suggested.

Supergranny laughed. "When you three broke up the party, Weird Sunglasses locked you in *THE* room. Then she probably grabbed the projector and escaped. Maybe she took the outside projector as well. Who knows?" Supergranny said.

"And who cares?" Angela asked. "As long as we stopped them ... *if* we stopped them."

Just then, we heard a commotion in the parking lot.

It was Bombast, his heels clicking briskly across the cobblestones. He was carrying his suitcases!

He opened the Mercedes trunk, placed both suitcases inside, and slammed the trunk angrily.

Then he turned and stared at us on the balcony.

For a second we all stared back. It was tense.

"Smile," Supergranny hissed.

Oma smiled. Angela smiled. Vannie smiled. I smiled.

"Auf Wiedersehen,"[1] Oma called.

Supergranny waved cheerfully. We all waved cheerfully.

Bombast scowled, then stepped into the Mercedes.

The Mercedes door slammed. The Mercedes engine roared. The Mercedes drove out of the parking lot.

"Yeahhhhhhh," Vannie whispered, clapping softly under the table.

"Don't 'yeah,' yet," Supergranny said. "We still don't know if he signed the paper."

"I'll check," Oma said. "After all, I've got to make up his room."

We all sat as stiff as posts as she left. If Bombast hadn't signed the paper, we were in deep trouble. He could call

---

1. *Auf Wiedersehen.* Sounds like "Owf Veder sayin'." Means "Goodbye" (Actually, until we meet again).

another press conference anytime, anywhere, and go on with his million-dollar scam.

We'd taken our best shot last night. If that hadn't worked, it would be forty times harder next time around.

Finally, Oma burst back onto the balcony, waving a white piece of paper. She threw it on the table with a flourish. "It was right on the nightstand where Jack left it," she said.

It was the statement Angela had typed in English on Meg's typewriter the night before:

"I have never met the ghost of Princess Elizabeth and have no knowledge of her diary. Everything I've said in this regard was in error and I totally retract it all."

It was signed "Otto von Bombast"!

He'd signed it! We'd won!

The statement was just a fancy way of admitting he'd lied.

Five minutes later the three publishers arrived, and Oma invited them to join us.

"Where's Bombast?" Publisher One asked, gulping coffee.

"I'm ready to sign," Publisher Two said, munching a roll.

"I'll double their offer," Publisher Three said, whipping out a gold-plated checkbook.

"I'm afraid we have bad news for you," Supergranny said. "Count Bombast has admitted he never met the ghost of Princess Elizabeth, and there is no real diary."

"Impossible," said Publisher One.

"I don't believe it," said Publisher Two.

"He's just stalling for more money," said Publisher Three. "I'll double my offer."

Silently, Supergranny passed Bombast's signed statement around the table.

"Ouch," said Publisher One.

"So much for rewriting 17th-century history," said Publisher Two.

"So much for the Ghost of Heidelberg Castle," said Publisher Three, pocketing his checkbook.

Oma brought out more coffee and rolls to cheer them up. It seemed to help. Before long they were laughing, patting each other on the back and saying "gootchie, gootchie, gootchie" to Baby Sadie.

We all shook their hands as they left and waved as they drove out of the cobblestone parking lot. As they turned onto the road to Heidelberg, Supergranny winked at us and pulled back the edge of Baby Sadie's blanket.

There was the corner of an old, brown book. She'd hidden it in Baby Sadie's blanket!

"I thought we needed at least one souvenir to take back to the States," she said.

It was Princess Elizabeth's phony diary ... the perfect souvenir!

20

Three days later, we left for home.

Oma, Meg, Rolf and Baby Sadie were on the Oberunterhof balcony to see us off. Oma was still waving Baby Sadie's tiny hand when we rounded the curve to Heidelberg.

We had one stop to make before the airport. We had to take Jack home.

His home, it turned out, was the Heidelberg zoo.

The day before we left, Herr Hinkel called to say the zoo had issued a missing monkey report the month before.

"It didn't dawn on me that night I saw him at the castle," he told Supergranny in German. "But the more I thought about it, the more Jack fit the missing monkey's description."

The zookeepers had figured Jack had run away for adventure.

"Balderdash," Supergranny said. "He was monkey-napped, that's what he was."

The rest of us agreed. We couldn't prove it, but we were 99 percent sure Bombast and Weird Sunglasses had spirited Jack out of the zoo.

"I know those two didn't treat him right," Angela said. "The night Weird Sunglasses dropped his cage, he ran from her like crazy."

That's how Jack wound up racing down the castle hall with Shackleford and me. He even dashed into *THE* room with us. *Anything* to get away from Weird Sunglasses.

The assistant zookeeper welcomed us at the Heidelberg zoo gate and led us inside.

Jack rode on Angela's shoulder one last time, chattering happily. In his excitement, he kept clamping his paws over her eyes and we kept having to pry them off so she could see where she was going.

As soon as he caught a whiff of the monkey compound, it was "Goodbye, Jack." He leaped off Angela's shoulder, scampered over the fence, and raced for a large rock pile teeming with monkeys.

Eight or nine other monkeys raced toward him, jumping up and down, hugging, licking and carrying on like a high school reunion.

"Well, he's sure sorry to say goodbye to *us*!" Angela said sarcastically.

We all laughed. It was really good to see Jack so happy. He must have been miserable being dragged all over Heidelberg playing ghost monkey.

We turned to go. "Goodbye, Jack," Supergranny, Angela, Vannie and I called. Shackleford barked her good-bye bark, and Chesterton blinked his lights.

"I'll bring you dried banana bits next time I'm in Germany," Vannie called.

And Jack, his arms around two buddies, looked quickly in our direction, raised his long, hairy, bony finger and waved goodbye.

*   *   *   *

We thought *we'd* had a busy week, but we didn't hold a candle to Carl.

He was waiting for us at the airport car rental counter when we turned in the Porsche keys.

A beaming, brunette, fiftyish German woman was with him.

"She's flying back to America with us," Carl said, proudly. "We're engaged."

Engaged! In a week! To an old girlfriend he hadn't seen in thirty years!

It took our breath away.

Supergranny recovered first. "Why, Waltrop, I'm so happy to meet you. Best wishes."

"No, no, this isn't Waltrop; Waltrop is married," Carl said. "This is her sister, Dagmar. We met last week and hit it off like that," he said, snapping his fingers.

Good night! It wasn't even his old girlfriend! He'd gotten engaged to a stranger!

It took our breath away again, but Carl didn't seem to notice. "Sadie, could Dagmar stay with you until the wedding? While we look for a place of our own?" he asked.

"Of course," Supergranny said. "Of course, delighted, of course."

She just kept saying "of course" and "delighted." She seemed too surprised to say anything else.

Luckily, all the hullabaloo of airport security and boarding the jet covered the awkward spots.

As soon as we boarded, Supergranny and Carl headed for the cockpit, and the rest of us stashed our stuff and settled down for takeoff.

We'd hardly sat down before Carl slipped back out. "I don't want Sadie to hear this," he whispered, "but would you kids explain to Dagmar about Sadie — the room behind the fireplace and all? I mean, Sadie is a lovely person, but as a visitor, Dagmar might feel a little overwhelmed. I tried to explain, but I can't speak German, and she doesn't speak English."

He smiled at Dagmar and kissed her cheek. She smiled at him and kissed his cheek. Back he went to the cockpit.

Next thing we knew, out popped Supergranny.

"I don't want Carl to hear this," she whispered, "but would you break the news to Dagmar about my office? If she's going to stay with me, she'll have to know. I don't want the poor woman going into shock her first night in America."

"But, Supergranny," Angela said. "We don't know enough German to explain something like that."

"We'll muddle it," Vannie said.

"She won't know what the heck we're talking about," I said.

"Try," Supergranny said, heading back to the cockpit. "It will be a challenge . . . something to keep you busy on the long flight back to the States."

Slowly, Angela pulled her German phrase book out of her tote while Vannie passed out the German-English dictionaries.

"I'll take 'magic snickerdoodles,' 'fireplace springs open in the middle,' and 'Stars and Stripes Forever,'" Angela said.

"Joshua, you look up 'southeast corner, helicopter pad and swimming pool.'"

"Vannie, you work on 'vending machine balcony.'"

Vannie and I groaned. It was hard enough explaining Supergranny in English. How in the world could we do it in German?

Dagmar just smiled, patted Shackleford, and dropped one of the gumdrops Supergranny had given her into Chesterton's cup.

"This is the captain speaking," Supergranny said over the intercom. "We've been cleared for takeoff. Please fasten your seat belts. Next stop, the United States of America . . . Heeeeeeeeere we go!"

ABOUT THE AUTHOR

Beverly Van Hook grew up in Huntington, West Virginia, graduated from Ohio University, Athens, and now lives in Rock Island, Illinois. A journalist who wrote for national magazines before turning to fiction, she has received numerous writing awards, including the Cornelia Meigs Award for Children's Literature and the Isabel Bloom Award for the Arts. She is married to an advertising executive and has three children and an Old English sheepdog exactly like Shackleford.

ABOUT THE ARTIST

Catherine Wayson grew up in Iowa and now lives in Huntsville, Alabama, where she is a full-time professional illustrator and free-lance artist and photographer. Her paintings and photographs have appeared in juried shows nationally and throughout the Midwest.